WANTED!

From the Fourteenth Wisconsin Cavalry, to the Texas Rangers, to troubleshooting for the Union Pacific—no place could keep Rawlins, no job could hold him. There was only one driving reason to live . . . to find and gun down the coward who killed his brother. Into the burning Dakota Territory Charles Rawlins pushed his search for a gang more feared than the Youngers or the Jameses—and for the man who murdered his brother with an ax. Rawlins wanted him . . . in the worst way. If he survived the Indians, the gangs and the gamblers, Rawlins just might live to see the man he wanted looking down the barrel of his blazing Colt.

WANTED!

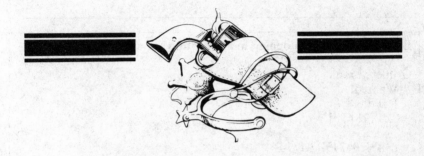

Frank Gruber

ATLANTIC LARGE PRINT
Chivers Press, Bath, England.
Curley Publishing, Inc.,
South Yarmouth, Mass., USA.

Library of Congress Cataloging in Publication Data

Gruber, Frank, 1904–1969.
  Wanted / Frank Gruber.
     p.   cm.—(Atlantic large print)
  ISBN 1–55504–862–5 (lg. print)
  1. Large type books.   I. Title.
[PS3513.R866W36 1989]
813'.52—dc19
                                           88–33003
                                              CIP

British Library Cataloguing in Publication Data

Gruber, Frank
  Wanted!
  I. Title
  823'.914 [F]

  ISBN 0–7451–9475–3
  ISBN 0–7451–9487–7 pbk

This Large Print edition is published by Chivers Press, England, and Curley Publishing, Inc, U.S.A. 1989

Published by arrangement with Donald MacCampbell, Inc

U.K. Hardback ISBN 0 7451 9475 3
U.K. Softback ISBN 0 7451 9487 7
U.S.A. Softback ISBN 1 55504 862 5

WANTED!

CHAPTER ONE

It was seventy-two miles to Fort Scott and the doctor intended to make the trip in one day. That meant leaving Cherryvale at dawn and riding the last few miles after darkness. Being a bachelor, he had cooked himself an unsatisfying breakfast, and when he saw the crudely lettered sign over the Bender's log cabin, *EATS*, he decided that he might as well have a substantial breakfast. Perhaps it would carry him through the day and he would not have to stop again.

Although he had never stopped at Bender's place before he had been aware that the left half of the cabin was fitted out as a crude store that carried a meager line of groceries and necessities, but the serving of meals was something new.

John Bender, the head of the family, was an uncouth, unpleasant man and Dr. Rawlins did not particularly like him, but the doctor knew that the buxom Mrs. Bender would do the cooking. And there was Kate, the daughter, scarcely sixteen but already showing promise of becoming a real beauty. The son John, Jr., was six or seven years older and took after his father.

Dr. Rawlins dismounted in front of the store. As he tied his horse to the hitchrail, the

1

head of the family came out of the log cabin store.

'Good morning, doctor,' he said in a guttural German accent. 'You are taking a trip?'

The doctor nodded. 'I left early in order to reach Fort Scott tonight.' He nodded toward the cabin. 'Is it too late to get breakfast?'

Bender shook his head. 'I tell my wife. You like flapjacks?'

'That'd be fine,' replied the doctor, 'and I'd like it even better if Mrs. Bender could give me a slice of ham.'

'Good. You have cuppa coffee while you wait?'

'Thank you.'

Bender went ahead of the doctor into the crude store. A canvas curtain had been draped down the center, partitioning the store into two rooms—one for the grocery section, the other for a dining room. The curtain did not quite reach the front of the cabin, the opening being the doorway between the store and the restaurant section.

Young John Bender, a hulking man in his early twenties, was behind the counter, arranging stock. He gave Dr. Rawlins a sullen look over his shoulder.

The elder Bender led the doctor into the restaurant where a long table was set against the canvas curtain.

There was a bench on each side of the

2

table. Bender asked Dr. Rawlins to sit on the bench behind the table, with his back against the curtain. He called to his wife, a stoutish woman in her forties, and gave her the doctor's breakfast order, speaking in German. Then he turned back to the doctor.

'You stay long in Fort Scott?' he asked.

'Only overnight,' replied Rawlins. 'Actually, I'm on my way to St. Louis.'

'*Ach*, St. Louis.' exclaimed Bender. 'Is such a fine city. I am living there from when I come to America in '47.' He shook his head. 'I don't like working for other people and always I think I get me a farm. Is good for the children.'

Kate Bender came through a door that led to the kitchen. She carried a glass of water and some tableware, which she began to set out before the doctor. She was a beautiful girl, only sixteen, although she could easily have passed for eighteen or nineteen. Much of the patronage that the store and restaurant attracted was due to her presence, and Dr. Rawlins, who was in his middle thirties, was well aware of her physical attractions.

He greeted her warmly and she replied with a shy smile. She started to leave the room, but the doctor called to her.

'Keep me company, Kate.'

She turned, her eyes going to her father for approval. The elder Bender nodded and went to the door of the store.

3

Dr. Rawlins pointed to the seat across the table from him. 'Sit down.' He smiled pleasantly. 'You're a very pretty girl, Kate, I guess you know that.'

'No sir, doctor,' replied Kate in confusion. She looked desperately toward the door of the kitchen. 'I think maybe Mama needs me, now.'

She fled to the kitchen. The doctor scowled after her, shook his head and leaned back, his head touching the curtain that served as a wall.

It was the last thing he did on this earth.

The blunt head of an ax smashed against the curtain with tremendous force crushing the back of Rawlins' skull. He fell forward on the table, his face striking the tableware, sending it skittering across the table.

Kate Bender, reappearing in the doorway of the kitchen, saw what had happened and let out a cry of anguish.

'Oh, no—not again!'

* * *

Later, after the Bender family had fled, the sheriff's posse unearthed the decomposing bodies of twenty-three men in the vicinity of the Bender cabin. The skulls of all had been crushed with a blunt instrument.

CHAPTER TWO

Three people boarded the streetcar at Division Street, but Rawlins was aware of only one of them. He took her dime and fumbled before producing the nickel change. Then he looked around and said, 'Plenty of seats in the rear, miss.'

She gave him a wan smile and walked toward the back of the streetcar. Rawlins waited until she was seated before he started his team of horses. At Goethe Street, he looked over his shoulder. She was the best looking girl he had seen since coming to Chicago two months ago. She was in her early twenties, perhaps twenty-one or twenty-two, five feet, four inches tall, and weighed about 120 pounds. She wore a heavy wool suit with a fur collar, her gloves were leather, with fur trim.

He looked at her again, when he brought the horses to a stop, but then was busy as more passengers boarded. At Chicago Avenue a drunk got on. He found a nickel with great difficulty and lurched against Rawlins as the latter started the team. Rawlins shoved him away.

'Sit down, mister,' he said in annoyance.

'How c'n a man siddown when the car's movin'?' complained the man.

5

Rawlins gave him a shove and the drunk almost fell, but reeled back and caught hold of one of the seats. He managed to plop down in it, muttering to himself. After a moment he drew a bottle from his pocket, took a healthy swig from it and seemed to feel better. He looked owlishly toward the rear of the car, saw something that interested him and, struggling to his feet, managed to negotiate a few feet of the aisle. A sudden swaying of the streetcar toppled him down onto a seat. He almost fell from it to the straw-covered floor, but managed to regain his feet. Looking across the aisle, he smirked at the girl who had boarded at Division Street.

'Hey, you're all right,' he said, cocking his head to one side. He doffed his bowler hat. 'I'm Corcoran, Mickey Corcoran, and I'm pleased to meetcha.'

The girl looked coolly at him and turned her eyes away. The man who had introduced himself as Corcoran was not too drunk to be aware of it. He scowled.

'I told you my name, what's yours?' he said belligerently.

She pretended not to hear him. Corcoran, still holding the bottle, took a quick drink and thrust out the bottle. 'Here, take a snifter of this,' he said. 'It'll warm you up.'

He pushed the bottle directly under the girl's face but she brushed it aside, using

6

more force than was necessary. The bottle slipped from Corcoran's hand, crashed to the floor and broke. Corcoran let out a bellow of anger.

'Why, you stuck up piece of fluff!'

The girl looked him in the eyes coldly. 'Don't you dare talk to me!' she said.

Corcoran blinked, but he was now drunk enough not to be repelled. 'Listen, you Halsted Street tramp, I've seen better girls than you—'

At that instant Rawlins whipped the horses to an abrupt halt and Corcoran was upset. He fell forward, toward the girl across from him, who struck out and slapped his face. Corcoran let out a roar of rage and grabbed for her. He twisted one of her arms, and the girl struck him again, with her doubled fist this time. The blow stung the drunk and he began to wrestle with the girl, but, before he could get a good grip on her, Rawlins had reached the back end of the car.

He caught the drunk by his pea jacket, twisted his fist into the material and yanked back and up. Corcoran came with the coat and Rawlins shook him savagely and began propelling him toward the front of the streetcar.

'There'll be no drunks on my streetcar,' he said savagely. 'And no rough stuff, unless it's me that's throwing off a drunken bum.'

Corcoran was not too drunk to take his

7

expulsion quietly. He struggled in Rawlins' grip and shouted imprecations every step of the way. But Rawlins kept his grip tight and, reaching the front of the streetcar, gave the drunk a final heave, hurling him through the door and into the street.

The drunk rolled over and came up against the curb, where he began screaming at the top of his lungs. Rawlins stepped down from the streetcar and moved toward Corcoran. He looked up at Rawlins and began to scramble away, still complaining about his treatment, but not as vehemently as before. A man who had been standing on the sidewalk moved toward Rawlins.

'Look here, driver,' he said, 'that's no way to treat your passengers.'

'The hell with you, mister,' said Rawlins and turned his back on the man. He was just in time, for the girl who had been the reason for Corcoran's ejection from the streetcar was just stepping down from the car.

Rawlins leaped forward and took her arm. 'I'm sorry about what happened, miss,' he said.

The girl tried to jerk her arm free from Rawlins' grip. 'Let go of me, you fool!' she said, angrily.

'Not until you give me your name,' said Rawlins, 'and your address.'

'I'll give you my name,' the girl said. She swung at Rawlins with her free hand, the gloved palm striking him squarely in the face. 'And here's my address!' She swung again, but he let go of her other arm and turned his head abruptly. The second blow struck him only glancingly.

'Whoa, now!' exclaimed Rawlins. 'You're a regular spitfire. I was only trying to help you . . .'

'Then drop dead!' the girl cried, and swung away from Rawlins.

He took a quick step toward her but was blocked as the man who had complained about his treatment of the drunk stepped into his path.

'Look here, my man,' the intruder said angrily, 'my name's Harold Carter and I happen to be vice-president of the streetcar company.'

'Oh, are you now?' exclaimed Rawlins.

'Yes, I am and I'm telling you right now that I don't like what I've just witnessed. I don't like it one bit. The employees of this company are carefully selected men and are taught to be courteous and respectable to passengers at all times.'

'Mister Carter,' said Rawlins, 'I'll tell you what. That's a good team of horses there and if you get into the car you shouldn't have too much trouble driving down to the horse barn on Harrison Street. Suppose you do that, huh?'

'You're fired!' cried Carter.

'Good,' said Rawlins, stepping past him.

The girl was a half block away by now and walking swiftly. Rawlins hurried after her. It took him almost a block to catch her and he had to call to her then, so that she stopped and turned. Her face was furious, as she saw him bearing down on her.

Rawlins chuckled as he came up. 'No use getting mad, miss,' he said. 'I got fired because of you and the least you can do is give me your name and address.'

'Why should I?' demanded the girl.

'So I can call for you and take you to dinner.'

The girl opened her mouth, but thought better of it when she saw the determined look on Rawlins' face. 'All right,' she said. 'I'm Molly Johnson and I—I'm staying at the Palmer House, on State Street.'

'I know the place,' said Rawlins. 'I'll be there, at . . . six o'clock?'

'Six-thirty.'

'Six-thirty it is—and my name is Rawlins, Charles Rawlins.'

She had made a complete switch by this time and suddenly held out her gloved hand. 'How are you . . . Charles?' Her grip, as Rawlins took her hand, was firm and he thought he felt a slight pressure before she withdrew her hand from his. She gave him a fleeting smile and, nodding, turned and walked quickly away.

Rawlins stood on the sidewalk and watched as she crossed the street and turned east on Grand Avenue. Then he shook his head and turned to walk back up Clark Street; but seeing the streetcar still stopped a block away, decided to walk downtown instead.

He hurried to Grand Avenue and crossed the street. Molly Johnson had almost reached Dearborn Street, but Rawlins began to close the gap, and when she turned south on Dearborn he followed, on the other side of the street. She walked all the way downtown and did not cross the street until she turned east on Lake Street, Rawlins again closed up the distance between them, and when the girl turned south on State Street, he moved up to within fifty yards of her.

He was not surprised when she suddenly turned right just before Randolph Street and entered the Potter Hotel. He shook his head in silent admiration, waited a moment, then went into the hotel.

She was nowhere in the lobby when he entered.

He headed for a uniformed bellboy who stood with his back against a pillar, watching the hotel desk. Rawlins took out a silver dollar, tossed it into the air and caught it.

'A very attractive young woman just came in,' he said, 'early twenties, a blonde. She was wearing a green wool suit with a fur collar, gloves trimmed . . .'

The bellboy rolled his eyes upward, emitted a low whistle. 'Mmm, yum, that'd be Miss Paxton. A real pip!'

'She's registered here? What room number?'

He tossed the silver dollar to the bellboy, who caught it expertly.

'Eighty-four, second-floor,' was the reply. 'Miss Lucy Paxton.'

Rawlins nodded and started for the stairs, when the bellboy said, 'She ain't in her room. She came in a minute ago, went out that way.' He pointed to the door leading to Washington Street.

Rawlins shook his head in annoyance.

Molly Johnson.

Lucy Paxton.

The Palmer House, when she was actually staying at the Potter Hotel. He took a turn about the large hotel lobby, then sat down in a large armchair, where he could watch both the Dearborn and Washington Street doors.

It was shortly after three-thirty and he waited. He waited until five minutes to seven, when she entered from the Washington Street door.

Rawlins was up and heading for the stairs, before she saw him. She stopped, showed instant anger, then erased it quickly.

'Miss Paxton,' Rawlins said, 'you're a bit late.'

'Oh, am I?'

'We had a dinner engagement. Remember?'

'I'm sorry,' she said, 'I don't make engagements with men I don't know. Not—not streetcar conductors.'

'I'm not *always* a streetcar conductor,' said Rawlins stiffly. 'In fact, I've been one for only two months. What if I was a—a banker, or a lawyer, or maybe a rich businessman?'

'No,' she said, 'I'm a working girl myself and I've been out looking for a job.' She hesitated. 'I can't have dinner but I will have a glass of wine with you. Give me ten minutes to go to my room and freshen up.' She indicated the wine room across the lobby. 'I'll meet you there.'

He nodded. 'Ten minutes?'

'Not more than fifteen.' She flashed him a warm smile and went up the stairs.

Rawlins did not go into the wine room, as there was a poor view of the stairs from there. He took up a better post and waited. He waited ten, fifteen and then twenty minutes and decided finally that he had had enough. He climbed the stairs to the second floor. Directions on the wall told him that Room 84 was at the rear of the building. He found the room after a moment and knocked gently on the door. He waited a minute, then knocked again, louder. There was no response from inside the room.

He knew that he had been had—again.

He descended to the lobby and found the bellboy with whom he had done business earlier. He took him aside and said, 'I want a key that will unlock Room 84.'

'No, sir,' said the bellboy promptly. 'That'd cost me my job.'

'To get ahead,' said Rawlings, 'a man's got to take chances.' He took a double eagle from his pocket. The boy exclaimed, 'Twenty dollars! That's as much as I make in a week.' He took the coin. 'Wait!'

Five minutes later, during which Rawlins did not take his eyes from the staircase, the bellboy slipped a key into Rawlins' hand. 'You found it, mister,' he whispered.

Rawlins waited a moment, then again climbed the broad staircase to the second floor and proceeded to Room 84. The key fit, and he entered a modest single room, furnished with a bed, two dressers and a washstand. There was also a tiny closet. Rawlins could see this from the dim hall light, but when he struck a match and applied it to the wall lamp he saw at once that the room had been hastily evacuated. Drawers were pulled out, the bed sheets were turned down. The closet was completely empty save for a few clothes hangers.

The little drawer on the washstand was also pulled out. Molly Johnson—Lucy Paxton had moved out, apparently through the partly opened window that overlooked the alley

14

between Clark and Dearborn Streets. A rope was tied to a large iron hook and thrown through the window. It was a normal fire escape and could have been easily negotiated by a strong young woman, very eager to leave the hotel without going through the lobby.

Rawlins carefully searched the little room, even getting down on his knees by the bed and reaching for the chamber pot.

There was nothing in the room except the hotel furnishings. No—there was something at the bottom of the wastebasket, some shredded pieces of paper, a letter torn into tiny bits. Rawlins dumped them all on the bed, searched the wastebasket and produced three or four more fragments. He sifted them carefully into a hotel envelope, which he found in one of the drawers, and stowed it away in his pocket. He spent a half hour in the little room, gave it a final survey and left.

He dropped the key to Room 84 on the desk before leaving the hotel.

CHAPTER THREE

The offices of the Pleasanton Detective Agency were on Wabash Avenue, between Madison and Monroe. The reception room was presided over by a heavyset woman in her mid fifties. She frowned at Rawlins' request.

15

'Mr. Adam Pleasanton is more or less retired,' she told Rawlins. 'He seldom sees people anymore. Mr. Billy would be best for you.'

'No,' said Rawlins, 'it's the old man I want to see. Tell him it's about Kate Bender.'

The receptionist regarded him thoughtfully for a moment, then nodded and rose from her desk. She went down a short corridor, knocked on a door and, in response to a voice inside, opened the door and entered the room. She stayed inside for a good three minutes, then came out to the reception room.

'Wait,' she said, to Rawlins.

She unlocked another door nearby and went into a room filled with wooden files. She looked through one of them and brought out a manila folder, which she carried into the office of Adam Pleasanton. She smiled at Rawlins and resumed her seat behind the desk.

After a few minutes she looked at a wall clock and nodded to Rawlins. 'You can go in now.'

Rawlins walked down the hall and opened the door of Adam Pleasanton's office. The old detective sat behind a desk that had seen much service. An open file was spread out and he was holding a sheaf of papers.

'How are you, Rawlins?' he said, extending his hand across the desk. 'I've just been

16

refreshing my memory. Sit down, will you?'

Pleasanton was about sixty-five and could even have been seventy, but his handshake was firm, strong. His hair was only iron-gray and his face, although aging, showed a strength that was remarkable. He was the most famous detective in the country and was now writing his memoirs while his son, whom he had trained, conducted the everyday business of the firm.

Rawlins sat in an armchair near the desk while the detective continued to study a sheet of paper. Finally, Pleasanton lowered the sheet. 'You're the brother of Dr. Philip Rawlins.'

'That's right,' said Rawlins. 'I arrived at the Bender farm two days after the sheriff found the body of my brother. I helped them dig for another two days and found some more bodies.'

'Twenty-three altogether, the greatest number of murder victims in the history of this country, probably the largest number of victims ever murdered by anyone, anywhere. An infamous family, the Benders.' He nodded thoughtfully. 'You know that I worked on the case personally?'

'Yes, sir, I'd heard that. I went back to Labette County two or three times afterwards. I worked on the case myself.'

'But you were no more successful than I was?'

'Not then,' said Rawlins.

'But now?'

'I think I talked to Kate Bender yesterday.'

'Here—in Chicago?'

'Yes, sir. She was registered at the Potter Hotel under the name of Lucy Paxton, although she had given me the name of Molly Johnson earlier.'

'The fact that you're here indicates that Miss Lucy Paxton—Molly Johnson is no longer at the hotel. Right?'

'Yes, sir. But I've seen her now. I know what she looks like . . .'

'About five hundred people in Labette County, Kansas, also know what she looks like.'

'But no two of them described her alike. I talked to fifty people and some said she was short, some tall, some heavyset, some slender. They guessed her age at fourteen, twenty, even twenty-five. Only in one thing was there universal agreement—that she was a very handsome girl.'

'That much I got myself,' said the old detective. He drew a deep breath and exhaled heavily. 'One of the few regrets is that my agency did not apprehend the Bender family. Nor did we even get close to a single member. However, I am a private detective for hire. I was paid for only three months' work on the case—by Labette County. As much as I would have liked to continue on the case, the

18

county decided that they could no longer afford to pay me and I withdrew. You, however, were on your own. And you had a personal reason to continue your search.'

'Unfortunately,' said Rawlins, 'I, too, ran out of money. I had to go to work to earn my keep. My last job was as a conductor on the Chicago Streetcar Company. I—I quit yesterday.'

'You've some money saved?'

'I have forty dollars in my pocket. The streetcar company owes me a week's pay, but I think I'll have trouble collecting it.'

'Why? It's a good company. I've represented them for several years.'

'Then maybe you can collect my pay for me.' Quickly, Rawlins told the detective the circumstances of his being fired. When he finished, the detective chuckled. 'I know Carter. He owns about thirty percent of the company's stock, which he never lets anyone forget. I've had words with him myself.'

He looked thoughtfully at Rawlins. 'Weren't you a Texas Ranger for awhile? I seem to have come across that information somewhere along the line.'

'I was with the Rangers last year,' said Rawlins. 'I served under Captain McNelly for about a year. I was a deputy marshal in a couple of towns in Kansas before that. Earlier, I worked for the Union Pacific, as a sort of troubleshooter. Since '73, well, the

19

jobs have been short-lived usually. I kept moving. Whenever I'd get a few dollars saved, I'd quit whatever job I had and start looking again for some clue to the Benders.'

'Where have you searched for them?'

'Where haven't I? I think I spent a year on the Rio Grande. I thought they might try leaving the country, for Mexico. But also spent some time in San Francisco, in Seattle and Portland. I've even tried up north . . .'

'But not east?'

'I spent a couple of weeks in New York, but that was hopeless. Besides, I'd come to the conclusion that the Benders would not have left the country. Old John was a fugitive from Europe, you know.'

'I know that,' said Pleasanton. 'I searched back on his trail, hoping to get a clue to him. Bender came to America in '47. He always told people that he was a political refugee from Bavaria, but that wasn't the truth. He'd killed a man there and fled because the police were looking for him. He came to America finally and settled in St. Louis, because there were so many Germans there and he apparently thought he could lose himself. During the war he enlisted in the Union Army . . . and deserted two days later. He was a bounty man. He enlisted because the War Department was paying a three hundred dollar bounty to all men who enlisted. That was a great deal of money to some people—men of the stripe of John Bender. He crossed over into Illinois, enlisted again, got his bounty and went on to Indiana and enlisted. Then he cut back, enlisted in southern Illinois, twice, then crossed back into Missouri. He enlisted again in Moberly, then moved west to Jefferson City, then continued on to Independence, where he collected another three hundred dollars and then made his last enlistment in Kansas City. That was a mistake on his part. It was too close to Independence and he was recognized and thrown into jail. He escaped . . . and took to the brush. He became another kind of soldier then, a guerrilla, and I have it on good authority that he was in Lawrence, Kansas, with Quantrill.'

'You covered a great deal of ground in those three months you were on the case,' observed Rawlins.

'I have many operators working for me,' said Pleasanton, 'but I must confess that it was my son Billy who made the only real breakthrough in the case.'

'What was that, sir?'

'He got me a picture of John Bender,' said Pleasanton. He riffled through the file on his desk and brought out a tintype, which he handed to Rawlins.

The picture was brown with age and showed a fierce looking man in his twenties standing beside a seated woman of about

21

twenty-five, who did not at all resemble the woman Rawlins had met as Molly Johnson—Lucy Paxton. But then the portrait of John Bender did not fit the descriptions of John Bender that Rawlins had obtained in Labette County.

'Their wedding picture,' said Adam Pleasanton. 'Taken in St. Louis in the fall of 1849. The photographer, Murdock, found the plate in his old files. The older Kate Bender, whose photograph you see there, was also a German immigrant in poor circumstances. Her father and mother had both died the previous year and Kate was working as a domestic—a housemaid for a St. Louis businessman. John Bender met her at a beer *stube* and married her two weeks later. Young John was born a year later and the Benders then began to move around St. Louis. He was an unskilled laborer, an odd-job man, mostly. He was a carpenter's helper, but he was also a teamster and for a while drove a beer truck. He was out of work a great deal. Young Kate was born in 1857, but the family was still very poor. They did not, in fact, know any real prosperity until the war came along. But even that did not last long, for when Bender began enlisting and deserting, the army officials began to harass Mrs. Bender and her children. In Kansas City, they actually arrested Mrs. Bender and kept her and her daughter in prison for a while. There's no record of young John during this period, so he was apparently staying with someone else, or shifting for himself, even though he was only thirteen or fourteen at the time.'

'Mr. Pleasanton,' said Rawlins, 'your secretary told me that you are partially retired.'

'I'm supposed to be retired altogether,' said Adam Pleasanton, wryly. 'I'm writing a book about my experiences. There's a chapter on the Benders, but I shall never be able to finish it . . .'

'Perhaps I can help you finish it,' said Rawlins earnestly. 'I'm going to get the Benders. It may take me another year, five years, maybe even ten, but I'm going to get them, sooner or later. Because I'm never going to quit.'

'I'm too old,' said Pleasanton. 'I don't have that drive anymore. My son Billy— he's running the agency now and he's got too many cases as it is. And the failure of this one case, doesn't bother him. Not too much.'

'I don't have the money to continue the search on my own,' said Rawlins, 'but what I had in mind when I came to see you—well, I'd like to go to work for you. On this one case, only.'

The old detective looked sharply at Rawlins. 'You expect me to pay your salary,

23

while you engage in a private vendetta?'

'Yes, sir,' said Rawlins promptly. 'But it isn't just my own vendetta. It's yours, too. Besides,' he added boldly, 'I've been told that you're a wealthy man and can afford a hobby. Let it be my pursuit of the Bender family.'

'Be damned,' swore the old man, 'you've got gall to talk to me like that. But damme, I like it and I've half a mind to . . .'

'I haven't told you everything, Mr. Pleasanton,' said Rawlins. 'I've a clue to the whereabouts of Kate Bender. The search may be a very brief one.'

He took a large, folded envelope from his inside breast pocket and drew from it a sheet of heavy paper. He unfolded it, revealing the tiny pieces of a letter that had been laboriously put together, like a jigsaw puzzle, and glued to a sheet of paper.

'I found this in her room at the Potter Hotel,' Rawlins said, handing the sheet to the detective.

Pleasanton glanced at the sheet of paper and looked sharply at Rawlins. 'Took a lot of patience to put this together.'

'Fourteen hours,' said Rawlins.

'You've touched up the writing, here and there,' said Pleasanton as he started to read.

'Yes, it was difficult and I had to guess at some of it, but it's accurate, I'm sure.'

Pleasanton began to read aloud:

Deadwood, D.T., June 2, 1876

Dear Sis,

I have a good thing going here and will soon have a lot of money. If you leave Chicago, write to me here, General Delivery.

Your brother, John

Pleasanton shook his head. 'About all it says is that your Molly Johnson has a brother named John and that he's doing well in Dakota Territory.'

'It's worth a try,' said Rawlins.

'If I were younger, I'd try it myself,' said Pleasanton.

'You'll pay my expenses?'

Pleasanton nodded.

CHAPTER FOUR

The building was not more than ten by twenty feet, a clapboard shack that had been thrown together hastily and held together mostly because the nails that had been used originally were good nails. Lettering on the window, read: *Westport Pipe & Tobacco Shop*. In smaller letters underneath was the addendum: *Capt. Tom Leach. Prop*.

Rawlins went into the shop, which was small and had a single, glass display counter.

A door at the rear apparently led into the living quarters of Captain Tom Leach. A robust looking man sat in a rocking chair behind the display counter, but as he got up and moved forward, Rawlins saw that he limped badly, like a man with a stiff knee joint.

'Yes, sir,' the proprietor said. 'What can I do for you?'

'My name is Rawlins. I talked to Colonel Harmon yesterday and he suggested that I see you. He said you'd probably be able to give me more information than he could.'

'Information? What kind of information?'

'It concerns the Blake Street Prison,' said Rawlins. 'Although Colonel Harmon was nominally in charge of it, he said that he was on detached duty during the spring and early summer of 1863 and that you were actually the officer in charge.'

'It's something I'd like to forget,' replied Captain Leach, 'just like I'd like to forget, my stiff leg—only I can't.' He looked sharply at Rawlins. 'You were in the war?'

'Fourteenth Wisconsin Calvalry, from the summer of '61. I wasn't commissioned until '63 and when I was mustered out in '65 I was a grade below your own—first lieutenant.'

'The Fourteenth Wisconsin was in this area for awhile, I believe.'

'Yes sir. From late '63 through the battle of Westport and a month or so more, before we were transferred east.'

Captain Leach nodded. 'Then you had a touch of guerrilla warfare.'

'More than a touch, Captain. Right after Quantrill returned from Lawrence, I ran into a few of his boys. I was still a sergeant then, but I had about thirty men. There were eight of the guerrillas. We ran into them just south of Lee's Summit. I thought we'd get them sure, because our horses were still quite fresh. But they didn't run, uh-uh. They charged us. They came at us with their bridle reins in their teeth and a Navy gun in each fist. They hit us and went through. We got two of them, but we lost six men dead and nine wounded. We took after them, of course, but they went into the brush and we lost them. They usually did that, you know—scattered.'

'I know,' said Leach. 'It was one of them that busted up my leg. That's why I'm drawing a half pension now and running this tobacco shop to get by. What'd you want to know about the Blake Street Prison?'

'My information is that it was a woman's prison,' said Rawlins. 'Relatives of, ah, the enemy . . .'

'Bushwhackers,' said Leach testily. 'Wives, sweethearts, sisters, two or three older women who you might say were mothers, but they were the worst ones of all and some of the guards called them something besides mothers.'

'There were also several children, I

27

believe.'

Leach hesitated. 'Twelve, if I remember right—and I do. Twenty-seven women, that is, all those over sixteen, and twelve children.'

'You won't like this,' said Rawlins, 'but what I want to talk about is the time when the building collapsed—'

'Let's get that straight,' said Leach harshly. 'The prison was a warehouse when the army took it over. Its location was a bad one, perched at the top of a ravine. The back end was shored up by heavy timbers. But the building did *not* cave in. Some of the relatives of the inmates deliberately weakened the shoring of some of the timbers, hoping that a section of the building would collapse—and they could get their womenfolk out.'

'There were casualties,' said Rawlins.

A bleakness had settled over the face of Captain Leach. For a moment he stared at Rawlins, then he nodded heavily. 'Three of the women were killed and four or five more were injured. Four children . . .' His voice suddenly became harsh. 'You still in the army, mister? A court cleared me once . . .'

'I know,' said Rawlins. 'I had a brother. He was five years older than I and had graduated from medical school when the war broke out. He was a surgeon with Sherman all through the war, at Shiloh, Vicksburg, on the march across Georgia. After the war he

28

settled in a small town in southern Kansas. In 1873 he was murdered . . . by some people named Bender . . .'

'Bender!' exclaimed Leach. 'I remember when the newspapers first came out with the story. I—I wondered if the Benders I knew were the same ones who . . .'

'Yes,' said Rawlins, 'it was the same Mrs. Kate Bender and her daughter. Adam Pleasanton traced them back.'

Captain Leach swore. 'Be damned! Mrs. Bender didn't get along with the other women because she was German and there were a good many Germans in the Union Army. The people out here, the guerrillas, used to call them lop-eared Dutch and I heard the term in prison. The little girl—she couldn't have been more than six or seven at the time—'

'Six.'

Leach nodded and went on. 'She was the prettiest one of them. Bright, too. I remember how she cried when her mother was hurt . . .'

'Mrs. Bender was one of the injured?'

'She suffered a broken hip.' He hesitated, then turned away from Rawlins and went to a small desk at the rear of the little tobacco shop. He opened one of the small side drawers, rummaged through it a moment, and produced a small ledger. He clumped back to Rawlins.

'I kept a kind of journal at the time and I

29

don't mind saying that it was a good thing I did. It came in handy at the trial.'

He opened the ledger and began thumbing through the pages. 'Ah, yes, here it is: "Injured: Mrs. Haley Matthews, lacerations of the face; Tessie Wilson, broken leg, bruises; Molly Johnson, bruises; Mrs. Kate—"'

Molly Johnson?' exclaimed Rawlins.

'The sister of the famous Johnsons,' said Leach. 'Bill Johnson boasted that he had killed more men at Lawrence than any other two guerrillas. When he was killed at the battle of Westport they found six pairs of human ears tied to his bridle reins.'

'How old was Molly, at the time of the—accident?'

'She was just a child, about the age of the Bender kid.' Leach hesitated. 'Her mother was killed.'

'How many Johnsons were there? Three?'

'Yes. Bill was the oldest. He was twenty-one or twenty-two when he was finally killed at Eastport and the leader of a group that rode with Quantrill. He was from Clay County and some of his best friends, or students, if you want to use the words, were the Youngers, the Jameses . . . Bill Johnson was the worst of them, but his brother Jim wasn't far behind. The youngest one, John, couldn't have been more than fourteen or fifteen in '63.'

'They survived the war? Jim—and John?'

'Who knows? They didn't come in after the general amnesty. I heard once that Jim had been seen in Texas. One thing you can be sure of, though, wherever they are, they're makin' trouble. The bad blood's there. Look at the Benders, the old man a bounty jumper, bushwhacker. The mother, the daughter, the son . . . ax murderers!' He looked sharply at Rawlins, 'You're after them?'

'I'm going to get them. It may take a while, but one thing I've got is time.' Rawlins hesitated. 'Do you mind if I copy down the names that're in that book? I'm going to check them out, all of them. Just in case Kate Bender or her mother kept in touch with any of them after the war.'

'You know,' said Captain Leach thoughtfully. 'You might be the one that gets them.'

CHAPTER FIVE

When Rawlins had left Kansas City the newspapers were filled with reports of the Indian atrocities in the north, but Dakota Territory was far enough away so that the average man on the street was not concerned. When the side-wheeler on which Rawlins had taken passage reached Fort Pierre, in the heart of the Indian country, he could not help being aware that the subject was now all-important. There were a dozen rumors. The Indians were out in full force. They had attacked this outpost, that Custer had taken the field against the Indians. He had somehow gotten out of his own difficulties and had resumed command of the Seventh Cavalry. At the fort, Rawlins learned further that it wasn't just Custer who had taken the field. The government was determined to defeat the Indians finally, and Terry and Sully and even Gibbons were also on the march. A giant pincers plan had been developed. The four armies were to converge from different directions, sweep the Sioux nations into a single group and there decimate them. There was little talk about trying to effect a new peace treaty. This time, it was to be a battle of extermination. Phil Sheridan was issuing the orders back in Washington, and Little Phil's antipathy to Indians was universally known. Although it was denied that he had ever said it, there were few who accepted the denial. They preferred the original statement: 'The only good Indian is a dead one.'

Fort Pierre had been stripped of more than half of its troops. Only a skeleton force remained to defend the fort, but no one believed that there was any direct danger this far east or south.

West—well, that was Indian country. The stagecoaches were still running to Deadwood, one hundred and twenty miles away and they were still carrying mail to points even farther west, in Wyoming, but passengers were being discouraged.

There was, however, a full complement to Deadwood—five passengers besides Rawlins. All were men and all carried guns of one kind or another, including Rawlins, who had purchased a Navy Colt in Kansas City. There were a driver and a shotgun man on the high seat, although the latter also had a repeating Winchester across his lap.

An obvious pall hung over the passengers when the stagecoach left Fort Pierre. There was little talk until a bearded, heavyset man finally expressed the thought that was shared by the others. 'Maybe we'll make it, maybe we won't.'

'They could have given us a cavalry escort,' retorted another passenger. 'Considerin' the taxes we pay . . .'

A well-dressed man in his late twenties bared his teeth in a wolfish grin. 'You pay taxes, mister?'

'I own property in Wisconsin,' snapped the other man. 'I pay forty-two dollars a year on it and that ain't all. I pay taxes on everything I buy, every pound of coffee, this suit of clothes . . .'

The well-dressed man chuckled. 'Well,

there's another way to look at it. Custer licks the Indians, the government can tax them—those that Custer don't kill himself.'

'They ought to pay a bounty on the Injuns,' exclaimed another passenger. 'Five dollars for every dead Injun and they'd soon be as scarce as the buffalo are now.'

'At five dollars a head,' reflected one of the passengers, 'I figger the government owes me fifty-sixty dollars right now. I've took care of that many in my time.'

'What's more likely,' said someone else, 'is that the government'll pay Injuns five dollars for every white man's scalp they bring in. Ten dollars for women's scalps.'

This statement was not received well by the other passengers and it was discussed until, finally, the well-dressed man, who was either a drummer or a gambler, singled out Rawlins. 'You ain't contributed nothin' yet mister. What's your idea about the Indians?'

'I think there're two sides to the question,' replied Rawlins. 'We've broken every treaty we ever made with the Indians. We guaranteed the Sioux that they would own the Black Hills in perpetuity, but the moment gold was discovered there . . .'

'You an Injun lover?' cried out one of the passengers.

'Not necessarily,' said Rawlins, 'but there's a right and a wrong side to everything . . .'

'I fit the Injuns during the war,' exclaimed

one of the passengers angrily. 'I seen what they did and I tell you there ain't a meaner, more savage bunch of critters ever inhabited the earth than the American Injuns, and the Sioux are the worst of the lot. I was in Minnesota in '62 when they begun massacreein' the whites—'

'Yeah, yeah,' chimed in another man, 'so the Sioux killed a few people, but they ain't the murderers that the Arapahoes and Comanches are. I had my share of them down in Colorado and Texas.'

The talk continued in this way, and Rawlins thought it was because the travelers were apprehensive about the trip they were making.

The stagecoach stopped periodically at relay stations, to change horses and to give the travelers a chance to refresh or relieve themselves. A longer stop was made shortly after sundown, when the passengers were given a rough dinner of beans and bacon, with hardtack and black coffee. Next came a discussion with the stagecoach driver about traveling the rugged mountain trail at night.

'I been over it fifty times,' declared the driver. 'I could drive it with my eyes closed. It ain't the road that bothers me and it ain't Injuns. They don't fight at night.' He paused. 'It's the road agents.'

'Road agents?' cried one of the passengers.

The driver nodded glumly. 'For every man

that digs an ounce of gold in Deadwood, there's another tryin' to take it away from him. Comin' back from Deadwood I been held up five times this last month and I even been held up *going* to Deadwood . . .'

One of the passengers pointed at the shotgun man. 'What about him? He's got enough artillery there to wipe out any bunch of road agents that ever operated.'

'I got my life's savin's with me,' howled a passenger. 'I was figgerin' to open a business in Deadwood and I ain't shellin' out to no road agents.'

The shotgun man shook his head. 'I never backed down in a fight in my life, except when the other fella had the drop on me.'

'The man takes my poke's got to kill me first,' declared another passenger.

'That's what he'll probably do,' said the gambler, 'especially if the road agent's Jesse James.'

'Jesse James!' cried the man who intended to become a merchant. 'He—he don't operate in the Black Hills.' He gulped. 'Does he?'

The stagecoach driver shook his head. 'I dunno. There was talk the last trip that Jesse's hiding out in the hills and if he's here he'll be tryin' to earn his keep.'

CHAPTER SIX

The pall that had been cast over the stagecoach passengers at the beginning of their journey settled upon them once again. They completed their meal and boarded the stagecoach for the night journey. Rawlins saw the furtive looks that passed from one man to another, the quick averting of the eyes when the other men looked at him.

As he climbed back into the stagecoach, Rawlins thought that, if a road agent were to stop the coach and announce himself as Jesse James, the passengers would be stricken dumb with fright. He wondered how he himself would react if he suddenly came face to face with the most famous outlaw in the country.

It was a long uncomfortable night. The road was rough, pitted with holes and frequently strewn with rocks that had fallen from the steep slopes. Rawlins did not sleep at all. Two or three times he was on the verge of dozing off, but always he was awakened by the jolting of the coach on the road.

The conversation during the night was desultory. Only the gambler seemed to get any sleep, although the others now and then closed their eyes. But whenever Rawlins looked at one of them for more than a moment he found eyes opened to return his gaze.

In the early dawn the stagecoach stopped at a relay station for a final change of horses. It was twenty miles now to Deadwood, the driver told Rawlins when he dismounted to stretch himself, and they hoped to make it at a fast clip. The mountain air was crisp and Rawlins began to enjoy the rugged scenery.

The stagecoach had traveled about ten miles when it started a steep climb where the cliffs on both sides seemed to press in close. The coach reached the top of the incline and began to pick up a little speed.

A rifle boomed off to the right. Inside the stagecoach the passengers became alert.

'Holdup!' one of them cried.

It was. Several guns banged outside and the stagecoach driver began sawing at his reins, yelling at his team to bring it to a halt. A horseman appeared, seemingly out of nowhere, galloped past the stagecoach and fired a revolver in the general direction of the shotgun messenger, who promptly threw his shotgun to the ground. He followed with the Winchester.

The coach came to a protesting halt. Horses swirled about the coach and one came charging up to the door. A masked rider thrust a Navy gun inside.

'Out,' he roared, 'every mother's son of you!'

Rawlins caught the eye of the gambler. The man shrugged, shook his head and began to climb out of the stagecoach. The other passengers followed, one or two of them complaining. Rawlins was the last man out and he took his stand at the end of the line of passengers who were being threatened by a man on horseback, with a very lethal looking shotgun.

There were five road agents. One of them supervised the shotgun messenger and stagecoach driver to get in line with the passengers. A third bandit climbed up on the stagecoach and secured the Wells Fargo strongbox, which he hurled to the ground with force enough to break it open. It contained only a few small parcels. One of the road agents began examining them, cursing all the while.

'Trash, nothing but a bunch of goddam trash. Where's the money?'

'Ain't none this trip,' replied the stage driver.

The road agent on the coach threw down the mail pouch. The driver shook his head. 'That's government property, mister. You take the mail, you get Uncle Sam after you.'

'He's after me now,' retorted the road agent.

One of the passengers managed to gulp out. 'Which one of you's Jesse James?'

'Jesse James?' exclaimed the man with the

39

shotgun. 'Who's he?'

'He's one of the Missouri bunch,' said another of the bandits. 'Seems to me I've heard his name before.'

'We're Texas people,' continued the man with the shotgun. 'We got a grudge against you damyanks and I want you should keep that in mind, when you shell out. All right, Sam . . .'

The man addressed as Sam produced a wheat sack from under his coat. He whisked it open and started at the end of the line, with the driver.

The driver protested. 'Look, fellas, I didn't give you no trouble . . .'

'You did you wouldn't be standin' on your feet,' retorted the road agent. He shook the sack. 'Dig!'

The driver reached into his pocket, brought out two silver dollars and a couple of quarters. He dropped them into the sack.

'Dig again,' snapped the robber.

The driver started to protest, then thought better of it and brought out a very flat packet of bills. 'All I got, honest.'

The road agent counted the bills. 'Eight dollars,' he said contemptuously, but passed on to the shotgun messenger, who sullenly produced fourteen dollars and some silver. The road agent cursed him but went next to the merchant who had talked about opening a business in Deadwood.

He moaned loudly as he produced a fat wallet. 'Hey, that's better,' chortled the road agent.

'My life's savings,' sobbed the merchant, 'eight hundred dollars . . .'

The next man along the line contributed a little over sixty dollars and the man following him came through with a paltry four dollars, which provoked the robbers to more cursing. That brought the man with the wheat sack to the gambler, who smiled cheerfully at him.

'I pass,' said the gambler.

'What do you mean, you pass?' cried the road agent.

'I've got enough silver to buy my breakfast,' replied the gambler. 'Stagecoach fare took all I had.'

A second bandit came forward and went through the gambler's pockets. He found a pearl-handled derringer and eighty-two cents, which he threw to the ground. 'I'll take the peashooter,' he snapped.

'Without it, I'm out of business,' said the gambler.

'You're a cardsharp,' snarled the road agent. 'Coupla fellas like you took me to the cleaners in Dodge and I ain't forgot it.'

He thrust the derringer into his pocket and moved to the man next to Rawlins. The man's elbow had already poked into Rawlins' side and Rawlins thought the man was so frightened that he would probably faint. He was weeping openly. The road agent slapped his face with the back of his hand.

'What the hell you bawlin' about?' he cried. 'All you're losin' is your money.'

'I—I haven't any money,' sobbed the man. 'Not a red cent. 'I—I was hopin' to make my pile in Deadwood.'

'You want to get to Deadwood, you got to pay,' snapped the road agent. 'Now, shell out!'

But the man only sobbed louder. Contemptuously, the robber went through his pockets and could find no money. He cuffed the man again.

'Never saw such a bunch of cheapskates in my life,' he complained. 'Nine hundred dollars in the lot of you . . .' He moved up to Rawlins. 'You better have some money, mister, or it's gonna be too bad . . .'

'I've got a hundred dollars,' said Rawlins, 'I've also got a Navy gun under my coat and I'm going to go for it if you make a move.'

The road agent took a step back. 'You reach, you're a dead man.'

'You'll be dead, too,' said Rawlins, firmly.

The horseman with the shotgun sent his horse forward. 'Mister,' he said savagely, 'you throw up your hands or I'll give you both barrels of this Greener.'

'You heard what I told your friend,' said Rawlins.

The man beside Rawlins let out a scream of

anguish. 'Don't do it, they'll kill us all. Give them the money.'

A second passenger bellowed out. 'You got no right to risk our lives.'

'You heard them,' said the man on horseback. 'You pull your gun we'll kill the lot of you.'

'Give them the money, mister,' cried the stagecoach driver. 'This bunch killed a man less'n two weeks ago.'

A general chorus went up from the passengers and Rawlins, in disgust, raised his hands. 'All right, all right.'

The agent in front of Rawlins reached forward suddenly. He whisked out Rawlins' Navy Colt, stuck it in his belt, then went through his pockets. He found the packet of bills Rawlins carried and dumped it into the wheat sack. Then he whipped out Rawlins' own Colt and smashed him along the side of the head. Rawlins went down. He was not entirely unconscious but for a moment he was aware only of a ringing in his head and of vast pain that lanced down, seemingly into every muscle of his body.

The condition lasted for several moments and by that time the road agents were all mounted and galloping away. The passengers gathered around Rawlins.

'You got off cheap,' one of them cried. 'You had no right to risk our lives.'

The gambler caught Rawlins' arm and

helped him to his feet, steadying him. 'At least you got spunk,' he said cheerfully.

'A lot of good that'll do me in Deadwood, without a cent,' said Rawlins.

'I lost every dollar I had in the world,' moaned the merchant. 'I've got to start all over.'

'We're all startin' even—broke,' chuckled the gambler. He winked at Rawlins. 'I'll get me a stake soon enough and you can tap me then.'

'There's a Wells Fargo office in Deadwood,' said the stagecoach driver. 'I'll see that the agent stakes everybody to a good breakfast. After that it's every man for himself.'

The passengers climbed back into the stagecoach and it was soon tearing down a canyon, on the last lap to Deadwood, which they reached in less than an hour.

CHAPTER SEVEN

Rawlins became aware of the burned-out trees that had given their name to Deadwood, before they reached the stretched-out Black Hills town that was said to have five thousand people living around it. Soon they began passing claims where miners were shoveling dirt.

Then the stagecoach rattled down a street that ran along the bottom of the canyon where Deadwood had been built. It was still early in the morning, but the narrow street was filled with wagons, horses, men—even women. It was as crowded a boom town as Rawlins had ever seen.

The stage came to a jolting stop before the Wells Fargo office. First down was the driver, who tore into the little office. The passengers got down and the shotgun messenger helped them with their luggage from the boot. By that time the driver had returned with the agent who was protesting over the driver's insistence that each of the passengers be given a dollar for breakfast.

'I do that every time a stage is held up, Wells Fargo'll go broke.'

But he began passing out silver dollars to the six passengers. Rawlins, about to wave his away, decided to take the dollar. The rough sleepless trip had made him hungry.

There was a two-story frame hotel next to the Wells Fargo office and Rawlins carried his valise into the hotel.

He stopped at the desk and asked for a room. The clerk shook his head. 'We ain't had a room in a week,' he said.

'Will you have one later on in the day?'

'No, sir, not today, not tomorrow. People're comin' into Deadwood, but they're not leavin'. Not until Custer wipes out the

45

Injuns.' He smiled brightly. 'That ought to be inside the next week or two, dependin' on how fast the Injuns run.'

'I've got to sleep somewhere,' protested Rawlins.

'Every room in the house's got at least two people in it, now. You want to make it three in a room?'

'Four,' said the gambler, coming up behind Rawlins. 'I've slept on a floor many a time.'

Rawlins hesitated. 'How much to sleep on the floor?'

The clerk thought for a moment. 'Two dollars. Then he added, 'In advance.'

'Road agents held up the stage, coming into town,' said the gambler, 'but I just sent off a telegram to Kansas City. I'll have a hundred dollars by this afternoon. In the meantime, let Rawlins and me put our bags in a room.'

The clerk hesitated, then shook his head. 'Road agents stopped the stage again, eh? Well, in that case . . .'

'Great,' said the gambler. 'I won't forget you this afternoon when my money comes.' He picked up the pen from the desk and signed the register with a flourish: *Marmaduke Higgins, Kansas City, Mo.*

He handed the pen to Rawlins, who signed, *Charles Rawlins, Labette County, Kansas.*

'Labette County, that's down in the southern part of the state, isn't it?' asked Higgins.

46

'Just above Indian Territory.'

A woman came down the stairs. Higgins turned and let out a low whistle, which the woman heard. She gave him a sharp look, then went into the dining room, just off the lobby.

'If there are any more like that in Deadwood,' Higgins said, 'I'm going to stay here quite a spell. 'Yes *sir!*'

'Uh, uh, mister,' said the hotel clerk. 'She's got a sign on her—hands off.'

'Phooey,' snorted the gambler.

'Her name,' said the clerk, 'is Lily Lane. That mean anything to you?'

'I've heard of it,' said Higgins, 'she's some kinda singer, ain't she?'

'Big time,' said the clerk. 'She's at The Golden Nugget this week. Then she's off to San Francisco.'

The gambler grinned. 'San Francisco's a very good city. I always liked it. Maybe I'll pay it a visit again.' He winked at Rawlins. 'How about breakfast, Rawlins?'

They left their valises at the desk and went into the dining room. There were a half dozen vacant tables but Higgins went past them to a small table where Lily Lane was seated.

Higgins pulled out a chair at the adjoining table. 'Ma'am,' he said, bowing.

Lily Lane looked at him and looked through him.

'Allow me to introduce myself,' said

47

Higgins, not deterred. 'My name is Marmaduke Higgins and this is my friend, Mr. Rawlins. We just got into Deadwood, after being held up by road agents.'

'Road agents!' exclaimed Lily Lane. 'That's all I've been hearing about since I got into this terrible country.'

'Awful, isn't it?' agreed Higgins. 'I understand the leader is none other than Jesse James, the famous bank robber.'

Lily Lane shuddered a little. 'Did . . . did this Jesse James get much?'

'Everything we had,' said Higgins, shaking his head. 'If it wasn't for Wells Fargo we wouldn't even be able to pay for our breakfasts. They staked us to a dollar apiece.' He smiled. 'If we had more, we'd ask you to join us, Miss Lane.'

'You know my name?'

'Of course. I was in St. Louis the last time you appeared there. I thought you were marvelous.'

'The Golden Nugget isn't St. Louis.'

'The Golden Nugget?' exclaimed Higgins. 'Why, that's where I'm going to deal . . .'

'Deal? You're a . . . a gambler?'

'There are gamblers and gamblers, ma'am,' said Higgins cheerfully, 'just like there are singers. You, ma'am, are a star. In my own humble field . . .' He shrugged.

Lily Lane seemed to accept Higgins' appraisal of himself. She nodded to Rawlins.

'And you, Mr. Rawlins, are you a gambler?'

Rawlins shook his head. 'I'm afraid not.'

'Then, what do you do for a living?'

'I've done a bit of just about everything. My last job was with the streetcar company in Chicago.'

'My favorite city!' exclaimed Lily Lane. 'You've sung there?'

'A dozen times. In fact, I was there only a few weeks ago and I believe I'm booked for the Palmer House again in six or seven weeks.'

A waitress came to take their orders, which she told them would be porridge, flapjacks and bacon, with as much coffee as they wanted.

'How about some fried eggs?' asked Higgins.

'We'll fry 'em,' said the waitress, 'if you fetch the eggs.'

Higgins grimaced. 'How about a piece of steak?'

'Not with the dollar breakfast,' was the reply. 'You want steak, it'll cost you two dollars.'

Higgins tossed his silver dollar on the table. 'That's my grubstake,' he said. 'But tomorrow, it'll be steak.'

'I could lend you some money,' Lily Lane suggested. 'Seeing as how we're working at the same place . . .'

'No, ma'am,' said Higgins, 'that's one thing I never do—borrow money.' He looked at Rawlins. 'Streetcar company? Now, don't tell me you were a streetcar conductor?'

'Why not?'

Higgins shook his head. 'I'd never have guessed it in a month of Tuesdays, the way you stood up to those road agents this morning. I would have taken you as a man—well, a man who's been used to guns.'

'I've handled guns,' said Rawlins.

Higgins regarded him shrewdly. 'The army?'

'I was with the Fourteenth Wisconsin Cavalry for four years.'

Higgins grinned wryly. 'I think we faced you at Westport. I was with General Marmaduke's Texas outfit.' He chuckled. 'That's how I got the name Marmaduke. My name's really Sam, but I took a fancy to Marmaduke.' He smiled at Lily Lane. 'That's a pretty fancy name *you're* usin'. Is it real, or did you get it like I did?'

'*I* didn't serve with General Marmaduke,' Lily retorted. She turned coolly to Rawlins. 'In Missouri, Mr. Rawlins, did you ever fight Quantrill?'

'How would I know? We lost some men to the bushwhackers and we got some of them, but we never took any of them prisoner so I don't know if they were Quantrill men or not. Why?'

'Because I—I've heard about Quantrill and his guerrillas. They were terrible . . .'

'All war's terrible,' said Higgins. 'But it's

50

over now. I wore a gray uniform; Mr. Rawlins wore a blue. We may even have thrown lead at each other. That doesn't mean we can't be friends now. Does it, Rawlins?'

'I've no grudge against Southerners,' said Rawlins.

'What about guerrillas?' asked Lily Lane. 'Former guerrillas, that is?'

'Most of them have settled down, by now.'

'Oh yes?' exclaimed Higgins. 'What about Jesse James, his brother Frank—and the Youngers? For all we know, they were the lads who took our money this morning?'

'They're outlaws,' said Rawlins flatly. 'Whatever they were during the war, they're outlaws now.'

'They claim they were driven to it,' said Higgins. 'Cole Younger's always writing a letter to some newspaper. I read one he wrote a while ago. He says the army drove him into outlawry.'

'He's a liar,' declared Rawlins. 'He claims also that he didn't join up with Quantrill until after his father was killed by Union soldiers in October 1862. His name and that of Frank James appeared in the Rebellion Records, as far back as '59. He was a ruffian and a thief then and he's still one . . .'

Lily Lane interrupted. 'A minute ago you said you were willing to call it quits against the Confederates—and guerrillas . . .'

'I am—against those that have settled

down. But the Jameses and the Youngers are still doing what they were doing during the war. There's another one of their crowd, John Bender—I suppose it was the persecution of the Union Army that made him murder twenty-three people, just three years ago—eight years after the war!'

Higgins suddenly snapped his fingers. 'Labette county—I knew that name rang a bell, when I saw it on the register after your name. That's where this Bender family murdered all those people. You knew them?'

'I never saw any of the Benders,' said Rawlins, 'but my brother was one of the twenty-three men killed by them.'

Higgins emitted a low whistle and Lily Lane turned to her food and began picking at it.

That was the end of general conversation. Lily Lane got up from the table soon afterward, bowed and went out. Higgins and Rawlins finished their meal and then Higgins said he was going to the Golden Nugget to try to arrange to work there.

'I thought you told Lily Lane that you already had a job,' said Rawlins.

'I don't think I'll have any trouble with Mark Mooney,' replied Higgins. 'I dealt faro in a saloon he had in Abilene a few years ago. I made plenty of money for him—and for myself, too.'

'I may stop in there later. I want to send a telegram for some money.'

Higgins exclaimed. 'Hey—I said that to the hotel clerk, but it was a lot of poppycock. There isn't a soul in the world who would send me a dollar.'

Outside the hotel, Higgins went off to the right; Rawlins turned left and went to the Wells Fargo office.

The agent looked up from his high desk, frowned as he recognized Rawlins. 'I gave you a dollar for breakfast, mister.'

'I know and I'll pay it back. As soon as I get the money I want to telegraph for.'

'You can pay for the telegram?'

'No, I can't. I thought you might trust me for it.'

'Wells Fargo doesn't do a credit business.'

'There's always the exception to the rule—like the holdup this morning. I didn't expect to get robbed while riding a Wells Fargo stage coach.'

'All right, all right,' snapped the agent, 'you've made your point. Write your telegram and I'll get it off.'

Rawlins took the pad of blanks and wrote:

Alfred Allen,
Box 203,
Chicago, Illinois
Robbed by road agents. Can you sent me a hundred dollars?

Charles Rawlins

He tore off the slip and handed it to the agent. 'This is to a post-office box,' the man exclaimed. 'It may take you several days to get an answer.'

'I'll get it today. My friend goes to the post office, twice a day.'

The Wells Fargo agent shook his head. 'I'll get it off right away, but don't expect an answer before late afternoon.'

'I'll stop by. Now, can you direct me to the post office?'

'It's in the Deadwood Mercantile Store—that's to the left, five-six stores. Mmm, six.'

Rawlins left the express office. He passed a restaurant, a millinery store, a photograph studio, a barber shop, a saloon and reached a building almost as large as a hotel. A huge sign running along the front read: *Deadwood Mercantile Company*.

Rawlins entered the best stocked store he had ever seen in his life. It was crammed with groceries, clothing, guns, farm implements, miners' tools and everything needed for survival that man could make.

A large cubicle at the store had a sign *Post Office* over it. Behind the counter, a prissy looking little man was sorting mail, putting it into slots.

'Yes, sir, what can I do for you?'

'Is there any mail here for John Bender?'

54

Rawlins asked.

'You John Bender?'

'I'm a friend of his.'

The postmaster took a few letters out of a slot marked B and ran through them. 'Nothing for Bender now.'

'There has been though?'

'How would I know?' snorted the little man. 'I don't remember everybody that gets mail here. Hell, some days I get a hundred letters.'

'How about Johnson?' said Rawlins. 'Molly Johnson—or John Johnson?'

The man regarded Rawlins suspiciously. 'What's your name?'

'Rawlins.'

The postman put back the B letters, took down a sheaf from a slot marked R. He shuffled through them, stopped at a letter. 'What's your first name?'

'Charles.'

'Yep,' was the reply. 'Charles Rawlins, General Delivery, Deadwood, Dakota Territory.' He handed a letter to Rawlins who was surprised, for he had not expected any mail.

He moved away from the post office wicket, tore open the envelope and extracted a sheet of paper. He glanced at the signature and saw that it was signed Alfred Allen, to which name he had just dispatched a telegram.

The letter was a brief one:

Have received letter from man who runs a tobacco and pipe shop. Says he remembered after you left that Molly Johnson became singer and now uses name of Lily Lane. Thought you might want to know. Good luck.

Alfred Allen

Rawlins read the brief note a second time, then folded it and put it away in his pocket. He started to leave the store, then turned back to the post office.

'That letter you just gave me—did it come in this morning?'

'No mail today, stagecoach was held up. Your letter came yesterday.'

Rawlins nodded and walked back toward the hotel.

He started to enter, then decided against it and went on to the Golden Nugget, which seemed to him a very large establishment for its type of business. It was at least fifty feet wide and almost twice as long. A huge veranda ran along the front.

Although it was early, the saloon was already open; it had probably not closed at all during the night. Rawlins climbed the short flight of stairs to the batwing doors and entered the Golden Nugget.

CHAPTER EIGHT

A bar at least forty feet long ran down the left side of the room. At the rear was a raised stage with a small dance floor just in front of it. The rest of the large room was filled with tables, chairs and gambling layouts of all kinds.

Two bartenders were on duty and about twenty customers at the bar and tables. A poker game with five players was going on at one of the tables.

Marmaduke Higgins stood by a faro layout talking to a huge, beetlebrowed man of about forty. Rawlins started toward Higgins, when the gambler saw him and gestured.

'Mark,' he said, turning to the man next to him, 'want you to meet a friend of mine, Mr. Rawlins, late of Chicago, where he was a big man with the Chicago Streetcar Company.' He winked at Rawlins.

Rawlins shook hands with Mark Mooney, proprietor of the Golden Nugget. 'Glad to meet you, Mr. Rawlins,' Mooney said. 'Hope you like Deadwood and decide to stay here. We can use some people here with a little capital.'

'Capital?' exclaimed Rawlins. 'I haven't a cent in my pocket.'

'That's right,' Higgins said, 'Mr. Rawlins

was with me on the stage this morning. We were held up and he lost all his money he had with him. Nine hundred dollars, wasn't it, more or less?'

'Less,' said Rawlins.

'That's our trouble right now,' said Mooney. 'The town's full of riff-raff. Every dang one of them afraid of Injuns, and just waitin' here until Custer wipes them out. Wild Bill Hickok's in town. So's Wyatt Earp, I hear, although I haven't seen him myself. And there's talk that Jesse James is here, although I wouldn't know him even if I saw him.'

'If he's here,' said Rawlins, 'he's probably got some of his friends with him—his brother Frank, Cole Younger, John Bender, John Johnson . . .'

'Hey,' exclaimed Higgins, 'you know them all, don't you?'

'I don't know if I do or not,' said Rawlins. 'I served in the army in Missouri and I got to know their names pretty well, but I wouldn't know Jesse James any more than you would. He's a name, that's all. A pretty bad name!'

Mooney, looking past Rawlins, nodded in the direction of the bar. 'There's a couple of salty ones, now. They come in here broke one day, the next they're spending it as if it was stuff they'd printed themselves. Only it isn't.'

Rawlins looked toward the bar and scowled. 'Put masks on them and they look like a couple of men I met this morning.' He started toward the bar. Higgins tried to throw out a detaining arm, but was too late.

The two men at the bar, who had just ordered whiskey, saw him approach. Both were in their middle or late twenties—tall, lean men, tanned from spending much time outdoors. Both were unshaven and wore rough clothes. Their gunbelts were conspicuous and each wore a weapon in his holster.

Rawlins fixed his eyes on the one who seemed a year or two older.

'Didn't I meet you this morning?' he asked, truculently.

The man shook his head. 'Don't think I had that pleasure, mister.' He spoke with a soft southern drawl that sounded like Texas to Rawlins.

'Fella carried a Greener,' said Rawlins. 'I couldn't see his face because he was wearing a handkerchief mask . . .'

'Whoa, mister!' said the lean Texan. 'You're makin' a big mistake. Me and Sam are cattlemen. We drove a herd up from Texas that we sold in Ogallala and then we come up here to see if we could double our stake.'

Rawlins looked at the second man, who smiled mockingly at him. 'What's eatin' you, mister?' the second man asked. 'You been robbed or somethin'?'

'I've been robbed,' said Rawlins, 'and I don't take it well.'

'You tell the sheriff?' asked the second man. 'Mebbe he can go out and catch the robbers and get your money back for you. How much you lose—eight dollars?'

'I lost a hundred,' said Rawlins, 'and a Navy gun.' His eyes fell suddenly upon the butt of the gun in the man's holster. 'Damned if it didn't look like this gun . . .' He reached out, caught the butt of the gun and whisked it out of the holster.

The owner of the gun had started to go for his weapon, but Rawlins' move had caught him by surprise. A look of chagrin came over his face.

'That's a damfool thing to do, mister,' he said, angrily. 'A man could get killed for it.'

'Give it back,' said the first man, 'unless you're figgerin' to use it.'

Rawlins spun the cylinder of the Navy Colt, tested the action. 'The gun's new,' he said. 'I bought it in Kansas City only three days ago and I'm not too familiar with it, but it does look like my gun and it feels like it.'

'Put it on the mahogany,' said the man called Sam, pointing at the bar. 'Lay it down nice and gentle and then I'm gonna beat the livin' daylights outta you. I hate to fight this early in the mornin' but if I gotta, I gotta.'

Mark Mooney came up, accompanied by Marmaduke Higgins. 'You fellas want to fight, you go outside, you hear me?'

'I hear you, Mr. Mooney,' said Sam, cheerfully. 'But a man can't always pick his own place to fight and 'sides, me and Joel here, we spend a lot of money in this here fancy place of yours and we figger we got some rights.'

He punctuated the sentence by suddenly smashing his fist into Rawlins' face. Rawlins saw the punch coming and tried to avert it but was only partially successful. The fist struck him a glancing blow on the jaw, upsetting him slightly.

He recovered his balance, tossed the Navy Colt to the bar, where it was caught by the bartender, as it slid across the mahogany.

He feinted a left jab at Sam, crossed with a right that caught the Texan on the jaw. It wasn't too hard a blow, but Sam did not like it.

'Not bad,' he said, 'not bad, but now I'm gonna kick the hell outta you, and I'm warnin' you right now, that we fight for keeps down in Texas.'

'You talk a good fight,' retorted Rawlins. 'Now, stop talking—and fight!'

Sam decided to do just that. He leaped in, took a hard blow to the stomach and crashed his fist against Rawlins' jaw. He reeled back from the blow and Sam waded in, catching Rawlins on the mouth, in the chest and again on the jaw. Rawlins tried to cover, but the Texan was all over him, whaling away with both hands. Rawlins had to resort to a clinch but Sam continued to beat him with his fists, hitting Rawlins in the back of the neck and in the kidneys.

Rawlins, recovering, shoved him away violently. He threw up his fists. 'All right, Texas, come ahead, now!' he said grimly. Then, without waiting for Sam to accept the invitation, he feinted with a left hand, catching the Texan unguarded, crashed through a right that caught Sam flush on the jaw and sent him staggering against the bar.

It was the last blow struck in the fight. The bartender, on a signal from his employer, brought a short-barreled shotgun up from behind the bar and fired it into the ceiling. The thunder of the blast stopped Sam and Rawlins.

Mark Mooney stepped into the breech. 'I don't give a hoot what you do out on the street. You can kill each other, but damned if you're going to smash up my place. Out—the both of you.' He stabbed a finger at Joel. 'You, too, Collins!'

Sam wiped a trickle of blood from his mouth. 'All right, Mr. Mooney, it's your shebang, but I ain't going to forget this . . .'

'The hell with you, Bass,' growled

Mooney. 'I've kicked better men than you out of my place.'

'All right, all right,' said Sam Bass. He gestured to the bartender. 'Gimme my six gun.'

'The Navy gun's mine!' snapped Rawlins.

Sam Bass turned baleful eyes on him. 'The hell it is, mister!'

'Then we'll step outside and continue this,' said Rawlins.

Marmaduke Higgins chuckled. 'My money's on Rawlins.'

Sam Bass repeated the name. 'Rawlins, huh? All right, Mr. Rawlins, the gun ain't worth fightin' for. Not when I got three-four better hawglaigs. Take the gun and wear it—and mebbe the next time we meet, when I'm wearin' a gun, we'll see how good you shoot. Huh?'

'That suits me,' said Rawlins.

Joel Collins said coldly, 'And if you're lucky enough to wing Sam—which I don't think you can—you got *me* to face then!'

The two men stormed out of the saloon.

Mark Mooney said to Rawlins, 'I'm afraid you picked on a couple of rough ones. They've got three-four friends who're as bad as they are.'

'They're two of the five road agents who held up our stage this morning,' said Rawlins firmly.

Marmaduke Higgins shook his head. 'You

63

may be right, Rawlins, but just the same, I wouldn't go challenging them. For all you know they belong to the Missouri crowd . . .'

'No,' said Rawlins. 'Both of them are Texans. I spent a year in Texas and their lingo is Texas.'

'Sam Bass, Joel Collins,' mused Higgins. 'I recognized the Texas accents, too, but I never heard of any Texans named Sam Bass and Joel Collins.' He looked inquiringly at Mooney. 'You said you knew some of their friends—they from Texas, too?'

'No, they're Northern,' Mooney frowned. 'These two stick together pretty much. Their story is that they brought a small herd up the Chisholm Trail and sold it in Ogallala, then came here, with eight thousand dollars between them. They claim they lost the money playing faro. Like I said, they're broke one day, flush the next. I'm inclined to go along with Mr. Rawlins—that they're the stagecoach robbers. We've had a dozen robberies since those two reached these diggings. Well, that's none of my business. As long as they behave themselves in here . . .' He shrugged. 'You ready to open a table, Higgins?'

'Just give me the cards—and the stake, Mark.'

Mooney signaled to one of the bartenders. 'A faro box, Al—and a hundred dollars.'

Higgins opened his faro game and almost

64

immediately had a player across from him. Soon there were two or three more and Rawlins watched the game for a while. He had played faro many times and liked the game, but wondered if he would play against Higgins if he had a sizable stake. Higgins was adept with the cards, sliding them smoothly out of the box, and placing the bets and raking in the money in swift, practiced movements. Higgins knew his trade.

Soon Rawlins left the Golden Nugget and went to the hotel, where he sat in the lobby for an hour. He dozed off but was awakened when someone spoke to him.

It was Lily Lane. She had changed her clothes and now wore a green velvet suit that reminded him of one he had seen only a week or so ago, in Chicago—the suit worn by Molly Johnson, who, Rawlins was convinced, was Kate Bender.

Lily was saying to him, 'If you haven't got the price of a room, Mr. Rawlins . . .'

'Oh, I've got a room,' said Rawlins, 'at least the promise of a room, with three roommates.' He grinned. 'I'll sleep so well tonight, their snoring won't even bother me.'

She was still looking down at him. 'What happened to your face?'

'I had a difference of opinion with a man named Sam Bass.'

'Who won?'

'We didn't finish, but I guess he had the

65

best of it, up to then. Except . . .' Rawlins
got to his feet and drew the Navy gun from
under his coat. 'I won this. It's the gun I had
taken from me in the stagecoach holdup.'

'You took that from Sam Bass?' exclaimed
Lily.

'It was my gun.' Rawlins looked up at the
singer. 'You know Sam Bass?'

She nodded. 'I don't know if this man is
really Sam Bass, but that he's a road agent, I
don't doubt. In fact, if someone said he was
the famous Jesse James, I think I'd believe
it.'

'He isn't James,' said Rawlins. 'He talks
with a Texas drawl.'

'You're an expert on Texas drawls?'

'I spent a year in Texas.'

'Where haven't you been? Chicago,
Missouri, Kansas—Texas!'

'I've traveled some, I told you that. But so
have you, Miss Lane. In your work, I mean.'

'I *have* to travel.'

'In your travels, Miss Lane,' said Rawlins
deliberately, 'did you ever run into a girl
named Kate Bender?'

'Bender?' repeated Lily automatically, then
looked sharply at Rawlins. 'Is she related to
those horrible Benders of—what was it?
Labette County, Kansas, who killed—'

'My brother. There were four of
them—John Bender, Senior, John Bender,
Junior, Mrs. Kate Bender and her daughter,

Kate. Kate was sixteen three years ago.'

A shudder seemed to run through Lily Lane. 'Why would you ask me . . . about Kate Bender?'

'You'd never heard the name Bender when it was mentioned this morning?'

'Of course I knew the name. I read newspapers, you know.'

'I wasn't talking about the last three years—since Kate Bender became famous. I thought you might have known her from years ago, say 1863 . . .'

'How old do you think I am?' exclaimed Lily Lane. 'In 1863 I was a child.'

'Yes, you were seven or eight, then.' Rawlins drew a deep breath. 'In 1863, Kate and her mother were in a women's prison in Westport, Kansas. There were other children in the prison, a girl named Molly Johnson . . . the younger sister of the notorious Johnson Brothers.'

'What are you driving at?' cried Lily Lane.

'Bloody Bill Johnson was killed at Westport in the fall of '64. He was one of Quantrill's men. He had a couple of younger brothers who were just about as bad as he was. As far as anyone knows they're still alive.'

'What you're trying to say is that Kate Bender and Molly Johnson were friends *then* and are still friends? All right, suppose they are? What's that got to do with me?'

'Molly Johnson became a singer,' said

Rawlins, 'a very good singer, I hear.'

'Mr. Rawlins,' said Lily Lane, 'go to hell!'

She turned and walked away from him. He started after her, but decided against it.

Rawlins left the hotel, walking up one side of the street and back on the other. At times, the wooden sidewalks were so filled with people that it was difficult walking. Deadwood was a busy town.

Rawlins counted a dozen saloons, although there were none as large as the Golden Nugget. At the north end of the street, he came upon a pistol-shooting contest. More than ten men were engaged in the contest and Rawlins did not know any of the contestants, but it seemed to him that the best shooting was being done by a gigantic negro, whom he heard addressed as Nat Love.

The contest was still undecided, however, when Rawlins went back into the central part of town. He stopped for a moment at the Wells Fargo office, but the agent shook his head. He passed the hotel and reached the Golden Nugget, where forty or fifty patrons were now in the big saloon keeping four bartenders busy.

CHAPTER NINE

Marmaduke Higgins' faro game had a full complement of players and Rawlins, after watching for a few minutes, concluded that Higgins was doing well. Several gaudily dressed women were now on duty in the saloon, talking to patrons, soliciting them to buy drinks.

It was some time since Rawlins had eaten breakfast and he was hungry but since he had no money he decided to return to the hotel and get some sleep.

When he got his valise from the desk, the clerk told him that he was in Room 6 on the second floor. He climbed up to it and found a grizzled miner sprawled on the single bed, lying on his back and snoring loudly, with all his clothes on. Clothing and packs were scattered around the room. Rawlins set his bag against the wall and stretched out before it. He was asleep in moments.

When he awakened he was alone in the room. The miner had apparently risen and stepped over him to leave. Usually a light sleeper, Rawlins had not expected anyone to move about in the same room without waking him.

He was still logy from sleep, but shook himself and got to his feet. His muscles ached

69

from the hard bed and his hunger pangs were stronger than before. When he got down to the lobby he saw that it was after four-thirty in the afternoon and he left the hotel and walked to the Wells Fargo office.

The agent grunted and handed him an envelope. 'Came through an hour ago.'

Rawlins counted the money in the envelope and saw that there was ninety-nine dollars. The agent grimaced. 'Took out the cost of the telegram.'

Rawlins nodded and left the express office. His first thought was of food, but he decided to pay another visit to the Golden Nugget.

Even before he reached the saloon, Rawlins knew that it was doing a roaring business. The clamor from inside was overwhelming and when he entered he could scarcely pick his way to the bar, where six bartenders were now dispensing their wares.

The stage at the rear of the vast room was lighted, and a man was doing an acrobatic dance on the little stage. No one seemed to be paying attention to him. His only musical accompaniment was a tinny piano that could barely be heard above the din.

Rawlins worked his way to the faro table where Higgins had been installed earlier, but another man was dealing faro now. Rawlins watched for a moment; but this man was not as adept as Higgins.

Rawlins was turning away when someone

slapped his shoulder. It was Marmaduke Higgins, with a crooked cheroot in his mouth. 'My supper break,' he said to Rawlins. 'And I've made enough to buy you your supper.'

'Thanks,' said Rawlins, 'but I can pay for it myself. My friend came through with the hundred dollars I telegraphed for.'

'A hundred dollars? My own mother wouldn't have sent me that much money. All right, I'll let you buy your own supper, but look—there at the bar!'

He turned Rawlins and pointed to the bar where customers were lined up two and three deep. 'Next to Sam Bass,' said Higgins.

Rawlins was surprised to see the suspected road agent back in the Golden Nugget, but he was even more astonished when he saw that the man next to Bass was talking to Lily Lane.

She was listening, with concentration, to an enormous man in his middle twenties.

Lily was wearing a low-cut gown of red satin, apparently in preparation for her performance. The huge man was bent close over her, talking volubly, now and then gesturing decisively.

Lily Lane shook her head in protest and spoke rapidly, which seemed to anger the man.

'Know the man talking to her?' asked Rawlins.

71

'Uh-uh, except that he's with the Texas fellow. They tried my game awhile ago. I beat Bass for fifty dollars. Man with him won two or three dollars.'

A ripple of applause came from the rear of the room. It rose in volume and became a thundering ovation interspersed with yells for Lily Lane.

The man with Lily scowled and stopped talking. As she moved away from him, a path was formed to permit her passage to the stage.

'Shall we eat?' Higgins asked loudly, his mouth close to Rawlins' ear.

'After we listen to Lily,' said Rawlins. He began forcing his way through the crowd toward the bar. The ovation and calls for Lily grew louder; when Rawlins reached the bar, Sam Bass recognized him and spoke, but Rawlins could not make out the words.

He looked toward the rear of the saloon. Lily had ascended a three-step flight of stairs to the stage. The whooping rose to a new crescendo, but as she held up her hands the noise began to decrease.

The piano player was pounding the keys and after a moment or two Rawlins could just hear him playing. Lily was still waiting for silence.

It came, finally, after an ovation that would have delighted an artist playing to an élite audience in Chicago or New York. At last,

Lily began to sing. She had a low, throaty voice that was hushed at times but, once silence fell upon the crowd, she could be heard even when her voice was almost a whisper.

The song was one that appealed to the audience in the Deadwood saloon, a ballad of a wandering man, far from his home, and of a girl who was waiting for him.

All play at the game tables ceased during Lily's performance and Rawlins, looking about, saw the rapt faces of her listeners. Here and there, he noted, a man actually brushed his eyes to clear them of mist.

He shook his head. The girl could sing, no question of that. Lily finished her ballad and the Golden Nugget rocked to the thunder of applause, whistles, yells, stamping. The audience wanted an encore, but Lily did not give it to them. She was there to draw patronage, but while she sang there was no money going into the tills of Mark Mooney and she had probably been instructed to sing only one song at a time.

She made her bows and curtseys and, ignoring the tumult, she left the stage. The ovation continued for three or four minutes before gradually dying down. There were still shouts for her and scattered clapping, when Sam Bass said to Rawlins:

'The little lady can sing, huh?'

Rawlins nodded. 'Didn't think you'd come

73

back to the Golden Nugget?'

'Why not?' asked Bass mockingly. 'I got money to spend and I can spend it.' He pointed to Higgins. '*You* got any complaints, card shark?'

'I will have, if you call me that again,' said Higgins angrily.

'You got a gun up your sleeve?' demanded Bass.

'I had a derringer,' retorted Higgins. 'It was stolen from me this morning. And I've got a damn good idea who stole it.'

'This the fella licked you this morning?' the big man with Sam Bass suddenly asked.

'Uh-uh, it was the other one,' said Bass, indicating Rawlins, 'only he didn't lick me. I had him beat when the barkeep busted it up.'

The young giant fixed glowering eyes on Rawlins 'You don't look like so much.'

'I had my fight for today,' said Rawlins.

'Yeah? Well, how about tomorrow, then?' sneered the big man. 'You want to waltz with me, then?'

Sam Bass began to chuckle. 'Yeah, how about that, Rawlins? If you had any money, I'd make a small bet.'

'I've got money,' said Rawlins.

'This mornin' you said you was robbed of every dollar you had.'

'I was, but I've got some money since then. From home.' He paused, then added savagely, 'From Labette County, Kansas!'

74

The name made no impression on Sam Bass, but Rawlins was watching the ruffian beside Bass and it seemed to him that the big man blinked twice. His lips parted slightly and remained parted.

Rawlins turned to Sam Bass. 'Ever been to Labette County, Bass?' he asked, then shifted back quickly to look at the big man. The eyes of the bruiser had narrowed.

But it was Bass who spoke. 'What the hell's so special about Labette County?'

Rawlins stabbed his forefinger at the big man. 'Tell him, John!'

The big man's lips moved, but for an instant no words came from them. Then he said, 'What the hell's this "John" business?'

'Didn't you say your name was John?' Rawlins shot at him.

'I never said nothin',' protested the big man. 'Fact, I didn't tell you my name. On'y—it ain't John.'

'What name *are* you using now?'

'Same one I always used. Bill Clark—' Anger twisted the big man's face. 'You tryin' to pick a fight with me? Because if you are, goddammit, you'll get your fight.' His huge hand shot out toward Rawlins, but Marmaduke Higgins, leaning forward, got directly in the way of the big man's grab.

'Hold it, sport,' said Higgins. 'Bass, I'm working here now and I don't want any more trouble with you and your friends.'

75

'I'm not makin' trouble,' said Bass. 'Seems to me your friend's the only one tryin' to make it. And he keeps on needlin' Bill, he's going to get the surprise of his life. And the worst beating any man ever got. I've seen Bill . . . fight.'

Rawlins surveyed the formidable looking Bill Clark; that it would be the toughest fight of his life he did not doubt, but he was committed now and could not retreat.

He said, 'Stick around, Bill Clark. We'll have another talk—and see what comes out of it.'

'We can finish it—now,' said Clark belligerently.

Higgins caught Rawlins' arm. 'I've only got a half hour left—let's eat!'

Rawlins allowed himself to be led away. He had eaten poorly the day before and the meager breakfast almost ten hours ago had not been sufficient for him. He had to be in condition to fight the big bruiser.

They had to force their way through the crowd in the Golden Nugget. When they reached the street, Higgins said, 'Never saw a man who wants to fight as much as you do.'

'I *don't* like to fight,' said Rawlins. 'I've had my share of fighting, but believe me, I never enjoyed it. Only . . . sometimes a situation arises when a fight is the only solution.'

'That business in Labette County—that's

behind this, isn't it?'

Rawlins sent a quick look at Higgins. 'What would you do if someone murdered *your* brother?'

'I'd kill the man who did it,' snapped Higgins. 'No question about that, but damme, if I'd spend the rest of my life looking for the man.'

'It just isn't *a* man,' said Rawlins, 'it's two men—and two women. I've got to get them all—but I've got to get one first, who'll lead me to the others.'

'What makes you think you'll find the people—or at least one of them—in Deadwood?'

'I came to Deadwood because I had information that one of them was here.'

'John Bender?' asked Higgins.

'He'd be about twenty-five years old today. And the description I got of him was that he was a very big man—unusually strong.'

'Well, that description fits Bill Clark all right,' said Higgins. 'But you could find two hundred men in Deadwood who'd fit Clark's physical description. Was John Bender also handy with his fists?'

'That, I don't know,' admitted Rawlins. 'The people in Labette County couldn't remember any fights he'd been in, but one or two of them saw him working around the farm and they said he was unusually strong.'

Higgins said, wryly, 'I guess he had to have

plenty of muscle to swing that ax . . .' He stopped. 'Sorry, Rawlins. That was in bad taste.'

'It's all right. Some of the bodies that were dug up were a quarter of a mile from the restaurant. There was one man who weighed over two hundred pounds. Took a strong man to carry a body that far.'

They had reached the hotel and went into the dining room, which was already crowded. The menu consisted of steak and potatoes or stew with potatoes. The men chose steaks, which were big and thick. There was plenty of bread and the coffee was strong.

After supper, Higgins said, 'I've made over a hundred dollars since this morning. If my luck holds tonight, I ought to make three hundred dollars more by morning.'

'What percentage do you get?'

'Half. The hundred is my share. Mooney's made a hundred, too.'

They were ready to get up from the table, when Lily Lane entered the dining room and came toward them.

'All right if I take your table?' she asked.

'We were just leaving,' said Higgins. 'If you like, we'll stay and keep you company. They'll be seating someone else with you, otherwise.'

'I'd like to talk to Mr. Rawlins,' said Lily. 'Alone.' She smiled at Higgins. 'Do you mind?'

78

'I've got to get back to the Golden Nugget,' he said.

'Good luck,' said Rawlins.

Higgins winked at him. 'To you, too.'

Rawlins sat down opposite Lily, as the waitress came bustling up to clear off the table. The waitress left after taking the order and Lily said:

'I've known Bill Clark all my life, Mr. Rawlins, and I can assure you that he is *not* John Bender.'

'Where did you know him?'

'In Rolla, Missouri, where I was born. That's in eastern Missouri.'

'I know. I was there for a while in '61.'

'Bill's a sort of cousin, a second or third, I believe. His mother was a Fitch, which happens to be my own real name, too. I was born Sadie Fitch and if that wasn't reason enough to change my name when I went on the stage, I don't know a good reason.' A cloud flitted across her attractive features. 'No, Mr. Rawlins, I don't have my birth certificate with me, but if it means that much to you, I can write to Rolla and get it for you.'

'Where did you start singing—in Rolla?'

'Mr. Rawlins,' she said carefully, 'I'm talking to you now for your own good. I'll deny afterwards that I told you what I'm going to tell you . . .'

'What's that?'

'My cousin Bill, Sam Bass, Joel

Collins—they *are* road agents, and they're a very rough bunch. Collins is nominally the leader, but Bass is as desperate a man as you'll find in the Black Hills. And you've met my cousin. Besides those three there are three or four more in their group who are as bad as they are. You can't fight them, Mr. Rawlins. Not alone . . .'

'I imagine there's a sheriff in Deadwood,' said Rawlins.

'There isn't—the county isn't organized. There's a town marshal, a deputy, but their authority is only in the town itself. What road agents do outside of Deadwood isn't their concern. That's up to the federal authorities and right now the federal people are up north, fighting the Sioux.'

'I appreciate the warning, Miss—'

'It isn't just a warning—it's an ultimatum. My cousin told me that Sam Bass considers you a threat to their group and that if you don't leave Deadwood . . .'

'I'm supposed to run out?' exclaimed Rawlins.

'Or else!'

Rawlins looked across the table at the singer, and a slow anger grew in him. 'They told you to tell me that? And you're delivering their message?'

'Yes, but only . . .' She faltered and stopped, then went on stubbornly. 'I know how it must sound to you that I'm an

80

accomplice. I'm not, believe me, I'm not. I was only thinking of my cousin . . .'

'A road agent—by your own admission.'

'Damn you!' Lily Lane said. 'Are you so blind you can't see? Who did I show a preference for this morning, when we first met? That tinhorn gambler? I've worked the boom towns, I've seen a hundred men like Marmaduke Higgins. But you—you looked like a different sort, the kind of man I—I might be interested in, in other circumstances. Damn you, Charles Rawlins!' Her hand shot across the table, gripped his larger hand, hard, but only for an instant. Then she withdrew it and leaned back.

Rawlins had time to reflect on the amazing turn of events, as the waitress came up with Lily's supper and a cup of coffee for him.

When the waitress left again, Rawlins said, 'I heard you sing. You . . . you were marvelous.'

Her mood had changed during the brief interlude; she had become light, cheerful. She said, 'I don't think a saloon full of miners, gamblers, road agents are the most discriminating audience in the world. By the same token, that song in Chicago, or New York, wouldn't even get polite applause.'

'I liked it.'

She said, 'I'm leaving Deadwood tomorrow . . .'

He exclaimed, 'Because of me?'

'No—I'm scheduled for Ogallala, in four days and it may take me that long to get to Nebraska. Then I go to Dodge City, and after that Denver and the southwest. I'll be in Sam Bass's Texas before the end of the month.'

'The way he's going, Sam Bass may never get back to Texas.'

'What about yourself?' demanded Lily. 'Do you think *you'll* live to a ripe old age?'

'I'll outlive the Benders,' Rawlins said harshly.

Lily Lane sighed. 'I think I've had enough of this stew. I've got two more songs to sing this evening, then I'm going to get a good night's sleep so that I can get on the early morning stage.'

She reached into her purse for money to pay for her dinner, but Rawlins threw out his hand. 'I'll pay for it.'

'No,' she said, 'I've more money than you have.'

'I'll pay,' said Rawlins angrily.

She looked at him a moment, then nodded. 'Thank you!'

She got up and started out of the dining room. Rawlins followed her to the lobby, where Lily moved toward the stairs. 'I've got another hour to rest. I'm going up to my room.'

'I'll be at the Golden Nugget.'

A frown came across her face, but she cleared it, smiled wanly at him and went up

82

the stairs. Rawlins watched her out of sight, then turned and left the hotel.

CHAPTER TEN

He walked back to the Golden Nugget, which now seemed more crowded than before. He edged his way through the heavily packed room, in the direction of Marmaduke Higgins' faro game, but never reached it. As he was passing a table at which there was a poker game, a man reached out and struck his arm.

Rawlins looked down at a grinning Sam Bass.

'You got some money you'd like to lose?'

There were three men at the table besides Bass: Bill Clark, Joel Collins and a man almost as big as Clark. He was an older man, in his late thirties.

Joel Collins exclaimed angrily, 'What the hell's the matter with you, Sam? That's the fella we had trouble with this morning.'

Bass winked at his friend. 'Me, I don't hold no grudges. He's a Yankee and I'd rather take a Yank's money than anybody else's.'

Rawlins looked around at the hostile faces and suddenly pulled out a chair and sat down. He nodded to the man he had not met before.

'What's your alias?' he asked.

'Alias?' exclaimed the man. 'What the hell you talking about?'

'Mr. Rawlins likes to pick fights with people,' chuckled Sam Bass. 'He's been sayin' all day that we're the fellas who held up the stagecoach he was on this mornin'. Claims we robbed him of a hundred dollars . . .'

'And a Navy gun,' said Rawlins grimly, 'which I've gotten back.'

The fourth man began to bluster. 'Nobody calls me a damn stagecoach robber . . .'

Bass threw out a restraining hand. 'Hold it, Jim. If he don't bother me, why should he bother you?'

'He bothers *me!*' snapped Joel Collins.

'And me,' growled the giant, Bill Clark. 'But I'm going to take him apart sometime tonight. Maybe tomorrow.'

'Are we going to play poker?' asked Rawlins, 'or are we just going to sit here and gab?'

Sam Bass began shuffling the cards. 'Jim—you don't have to shake hands with him, but this is Rawlins. Rawlins, Jim Berry. He's from Missouri, but he shore as hell wasn't a Yankee, during the war.'

'That I would have bet on,' retorted Rawlins.

'You're asking for it,' snarled the man named Jim Berry.

'You're after me,' said Bill Clark. 'I got first dibs on him.'

Sam Bass began dealing out the cards. 'Five car stud, deuces wild . . .'

'Deuces wild,' exclaimed Rawlins. 'What kind of poker is that?'

'In Texas we like a fast game,' said Sam Bass. ''Sides, it's dealer's choice. You're high, Mr. Rawlins, with the ace. Bet it . . .'

Rawlins pulled out his entire roll of bills, ninety-seven dollars. He peeled off two one-dollar bills and stuck them into his pocket. 'My room rent, for tonight.'

'We don't play for small change,' said Bass.

'All right, I'll open for five dollars, then. Let's see if you'll stay.'

Sam Bass had a trey showing and had not even looked at his hole card. He tossed a five-dollar gold piece into the pot. Bill Clark had a king showing and put in five dollars, after some hesitation. Both Berry and Collins studied their hole cards before donating the ante.

Peeking at his own hole card Rawlins saw that he had a deuce.

Bass dealt a second round and gave Rawlins a king. He was still high and bet another five dollars.

Bass, with a three and seven showing, threw in ten dollars. 'We'll see where the strength is.' The other players put in their ten dollars, none too cheerfully, but Rawlins counted out fifteen dollars. 'Ten dollars back to you.'

'Oh, you get the ace backed up?' said Bass pleasantly. 'Well, I don't mind tellin' you that I got me a little one in the hole and if I connect, it's three of a kind . . .'

Berry dropped out of the last raise, but Collins and Clark both called. Bass dealt the fourth card, a king to Rawlins, which gave him a pair showing, but with the deuce in the hole, three kings.

Bass gave himself a deuce up and explained, 'Just the baby I wanted. All right, Rawlins, you got the big pair. Bet her.'

'I'll check to you.'

'Well, we'll see what you got. Twenty dollars.'

Collins put in twenty with ill grace, and Clark dropped out. Rawlins put in twenty dollars. 'I'll call.'

'Two pair, hey?' exclaimed Bass.

He dealt the final card to Rawlins, a deuce, then gave himself another two. Collins received a queen and turned down his hand.

'Well, well, well!' cried Bass. 'Looks like we got us a full house. Go ahead, bet her . . .'

'You're trying to tell me that you've got four of a kind,' said Rawlins.

'Pay and find out the bad news.'

'We're playing table stakes I imagine,' said Rawlins. 'I've got exactly fifty-five dollars left. I'll bet it.'

Bass's good humor vanished for a moment. He leaned forward and studied Rawlins' hand. 'You didn't bet it like you had it,' he said. 'I think you're trying to make your full house stand up against my four sevens.' He began handling his money, which was not much more than Rawlins' remaining stake. 'Two deuces showing and I got one in the hole. Chances are you haven't got the fourth one . . .'

'Fifty-five dollars,' said Rawlins.

'I still think you're bluffing.' Bass scowled then pushed out fifty-five dollars. 'I've really got my deuce,' he said, turning it up.

'I really got mine,' said Rawlins and reached out to gather up the pot.

Bass banged his fist on the table. 'You're either the worst poker player I've ever seen—or you're smarter than I figured you for.'

'Mr. Collins,' said Rawlins, 'it's your deal.'

Collins swore. 'I'm down to thirty dollars, after that hand . . .'

'What're you complaining about?' snapped Bass. 'After that damn faro dealer got through with me . . .'

'You've got eighteen dollars, there,' said Rawlins. 'I'll cut you high card for it.'

'I've got a roll back at the shack. I'll play light . . .'

'Not with me you won't. If it's all the same with the rest of you we'll play one showdown hand, the cards up, for eighteen dollars. Then, if Mr. Bass loses, he can drop out. If he wins we'll play a showdown hand for thirty-six dollars.'

'Keep talking,' snarled Bass, 'and I'll turn Clark loose on you now . . .'

'I'm ready,' volunteered the giant.

'All right,' said Collins, angrily, 'showdown it'll be—for eighteen dollars.'

He dealt the cards swiftly, face up. After the second card, Bass had a pair of tens and was beginning to smirk again, but his hand did not improve after that. Jim Berry got himself a pair of kings on the third card and Rawlins got an ace, which was of no advantage since no other card was close.

On the fourth card, Collins had a pair of fours, but Rawlins' hand did not improve.

'Last card,' announced Collins. He dealt an inconsequential card to Berry, which did not help the Missourian. He gave Clark an ace, which gave him a pair of kings, ace high. The next card was to Rawlins—and it was another ace, which gave him a pair. Bass caught an ace and he swore roundly. Collins as dealer was the last man and he held up the card for a moment before he turned it up.

'You win, Mr. Rawlins,' he said, bitterly.

'You're a lucky bastard,' snarled Bass.

'I work for my money,' said Rawlins, 'you don't. You can always hold up another stagecoach. Incidentally, there are two tomorrow morning, one coming in, one going out. By good timing you can get them both . . .'

'Bill,' said Bass, nastily. 'I ain't goin' to hold you back no more. You want him, he's yours . . .'

Bill Clark pushed back his chair and got to his feet. 'You want it in here, Rawlins, or do we go outside, where I can have fighting room?'

At that moment, a whiskered man wearing a badge on his calico shirt slammed open the batwing doors of the Golden Nugget. He held a .45 revolver in his fist, which he pointed at the ceiling—and fired.

He turned to a man who had come in on his heels, obviously an Indian, although he wore remnants of a cavalry uniform. 'Listen to this, folks!' he shouted. 'This man just come from the battlefield.' He fired his .45 again, then bellowed out:

'Custer's been licked!'

A thunderous roar went up in the huge saloon. Men began to yell and curse, and the town's marshal had to fire his revolver into the ceiling twice more before he got some quiet.

'This man's Winded Horse, a Crow scout who's been with Custer. He rode here in twenty-two hours from the Little Big Horn, where Custer got licked. He thinks they're all wiped out, the whole Seventh Cavalry, but he didn't wait to find out for sure. There was too damned many Injuns around!'

'Custer's a damn Yank,' swore Sam Bass, 'but he was down in Texas after the war. No damn Injun ever licked him.'

'You're a Yank yourself, Sam,' snapped Joel Collins. 'You on'y come to Texas after the war. You're still a Hoosier at heart. The only way Custer could ever lick Injuns was like he done at the Washita, catch 'em in the snow, the women and kids with them. The Sioux are horse fighters. Custer never saw the day he could lick them . . .'

Jim Berry offered: 'We'd have him in Missouri durin' the war, we'd have beat the tar out of him.'

Rawlins had finished gathering together his money. He stowed it away in a pocket and rose to his feet. He nodded and moved away and none of the road agents tried to stop him. They were now too engrossed with the tragedy that had befallen the great Custer, although of the group, only Sam Bass was defending Custer.

All play in the saloon seemed to be suspended and Mark Mooney, the proprietor, moved toward the pianist to get him to play, so that the spell would be broken. Customers began to leave; those that remained crowded around the marshal and the Indian scout, or jabbered away excitedly about Custer. Some were loath to believe the news. Others were only too prone to accept—and magnify—it. Soon the rumor ran through the crowd that every man of the Seventh Cavalry, including Custer himself, had been killed. Others added that all the soldiers in Montana had been defeated, the troops of Sully, Gibbon and Terry. A pall settled upon the saloon, which was not broken when the comic dancer appeared on the stage and began a furious buck-and-wing. No one paid any attention to him.

It would have taken Lily Lane to restore the spirits of this crowd and Lily Lane was at the hotel, preparing for a later appearance.

Rawlins moved to Higgins' faro layout, where all play had stopped. The glum Higgins looked up at him.

'You believe it?' he asked.

'I don't know. The Indian didn't say he actually saw the battle. It may be just another rumor.'

'If it's true,' said Higgins heavily, 'this town's dead. There'll be a stampede away from here. I may not even wait for it, though, the way things have been going for me.'

'I thought you were winning?'

'My luck turned after supper. I've lost all I won—and most of Mooney's stake.'

'Bass said he dropped a wad playing faro.'

'Not at this table, he didn't. I saw you playing poker with him. You do all right?'

'Very good. Bass is flat broke and so's Collins.'

'They can always hold up another

91

stagecoach.'

'That's what I told them.'

'You don't stop, do you?'

'Bass was just telling Clark to go for me, when the marshal came in with the Indian. Saved a fight.'

'Then don't press your luck anymore. Not tonight.'

'I've got to fight Clark,' said Rawlins, 'and I've got to beat him. It's the only way I can make him talk.'

'Talk, talk!' exclaimed Higgins irritably. 'About what? The man's a giant oaf, that's all. He's no more John Bender than I am.' He stopped as Rawlins looked down at him coolly. 'Sorry, Rawlins. I'm not a good loser. Deadwood's been no good for me and if I go broke tonight, I'm pulling out tomorrow. Along with about three-fourths of the population, I guess . . .'

Lily Lane, accompanied by one of the bartenders, was coming through the door. 'Mooney's sent for Lily,' Rawlins observed. 'He's going to try to liven things up.'

He was right, for Mooney went to meet Lily and talked animatedly to her as they went back toward the stage. As she climbed the short flight of steps, the pianist began to play and Mooney roared above the noise of the saloon:

'Gentlemen! I give you again—Miss Lily Lane!'

The pianist switched into 'Buffalo Gals' and Lily Lane was singing the lively frontier tune. But while she sang, men were still talking in the saloon; it was not as it had been earlier in the evening.

CHAPTER ELEVEN

Lily sang loudly and brightly, but the hum of talk did not stop. She finished 'Buffalo Gals,' signaled to the piano player and again sang the haunting ballad with which she had enthralled the audience earlier.

It did not have the same effect this time. Talk still continued and men kept leaving the saloon. She finished the second song to a desultory handclapping of a dozen or so miners. The Golden Nugget was less than half full when Lily left the stage. Mooney tried to get her to go back for a third song, but she refused and came toward Higgins and Rawlins.

'Lily Lane,' she said to Rawlins, 'flopsinger!'

'You can't sing against Custer,' said Rawlins.

'You think he's really dead?'

'If he is,' said Rawlins, 'it's the worst catastrophe that ever hit the West. Fetterman had only a hundred men with him when he

93

was wiped out, but look at the effect of that massacre.' He shook his head. 'I can't believe that Custer with six hundred or seven hundred crack cavalry was beaten by a handful of Indians . . .'

'Handful?' exclaimed Higgins. 'Twenty different Sioux tribes went on the warpath. They could raise twenty or thirty thousand fighting men.'

'They never have before. Even in '62 they didn't have more than eight thousand men in the field and that was the largest number they've ever put together at any one time.'

Higgins pushed back his cushioned chair and got to his feet. 'There's going to be a scramble for tickets on the stagecoach, as soon as they get time to think. I'm going over now and book my passage—while I've still got a few dollars left.'

'You're leaving Deadwood, Mr. Higgins?' exclaimed Lily.

Higgins nodded. 'It's going to be as dead as its name. You've got a stake, Rawlins—you coming with me?'

'No,' said Rawlins, 'I don't think I will.'

'I didn't think you would.' Higgins touched Lily's arm. 'I'll walk you to the hotel.'

There was a cloud on Lily's face as she looked at Rawlins, but she left the saloon with Higgins.

Looking around, Rawlins saw the road

agents still at their table. He walked toward them. Bill Clark rose belligerently. 'We gonna have that fight now?'

'I'm not in the mood now,' snapped Rawlins. He nodded to Sam Bass. 'You boys got horses?'

'I'm from Texas,' said Bass. 'I've got a horse—naturally.'

'I'd like to buy one from you.'

'I've got a deal with the livery stable,' retorted Bass. 'I don't sell horses, they don't hold up stagecoaches.'

'Damn it, Sam,' swore Collins, 'that joking of yours is going to get you into trouble one of these days.'

'Who's joking?' said Bass. 'You know I haven't got a horse to sell.'

'I'll pay a hundred dollars for a horse,' said Rawlins, 'which is about ninety dollars more than they're worth in Texas.'

'What'll you pay with—the money you won from me?' exclaimed Bass.

'I'll pay cash. What difference does it make how I got the money? A hundred and fifty dollars for a *good* horse.'

Sam Bass stared at him. Then he drew a deep breath. 'Two hundred dollars and you got yourself a horse, mister.'

'We've only got one extra mount, Sam,' protested Joel Collins.

'All right—we'll take two hundred dollars for her. Cash.'

'I won't let you sell, Sam,' said Joel Collins.

'The hell you won't,' replied Bass. 'We need the grubstake. Hand over the two hundred and the nag's your'n.'

'I'll give you the money when I get the horse.'

Sam Bass got to his feet. 'Come on, it's five minutes' walk from here.'

Bill Clark got quickly to his feet. 'I'll go with you.' He grinned wickedly.

'It takes only one man to sell a horse,' said Rawlins. 'I'll go with Bass—alone.'

'We need the money,' Sam Bass said simply.

Collins made no further protest, and Bass and Rawlins left the Golden Nugget together. Outside, Bass led the way to the south end of the street and into the open space beyond it. As Rawlins walked beside him, Bass said, 'You're a pretty tough character, Rawlins. I wouldn't mind havin' a man like you backin' me in the clinches.'

'I wouldn't be any good holding up stagecoaches.'

'I'm quittin' that penny ante stuff,' replied Bass. 'Hell, last week we held up a stage coach and come away with fourteen dollars.'

'You made more this morning—over nine hundred dollars.'

'And it's gone, every dollar of it. I keep tellin' Joel it ain't worth the effort. What we

96

need's one big job, the kinda haul Jesse James gets.'

'Isn't there a report that he's here in Deadwood?' asked Rawlins.

'He is, he ain't showin' hisself. 'Course I wouldn't know him from Adam, but Jim Berry claims he knows him real well. Says he rode with him durin' the war.'

'Berry was with Quantrill?'

'That's what he says, but he's such a danged liar I don't know half what to believe.'

'He's old enough.'

'What the hell's age got to do with it? Me, I'm twenty-six. I wasn't in the war, but they say Jesse's on'y my age, mebbe a year older, and he was with Quantrill. Joined up before he was sixteen. I was still in Indiana when I was sixteen. Workin' on a farm. Would you believe I was actually a deputy sheriff in Texas?'

'Would you believe I was a Texas Ranger?' asked Rawlins.

'Oh, come off it.'

'If you were a deputy sheriff, I was a Texas Ranger.'

Bass lapsed into silence for a moment, then looked shrewdly at Rawlins. 'Was you a Ranger?'

'I was,' said Rawlins.

'Well, I was a deputy,' said Bass. 'I used to work for the sheriff at Denton. He fired me,

97

after I began racin' my mare.'

'I never heard of a Texan who didn't like racing,' said Rawlins.

Sam Bass chuckled. 'I guess it was the way I won the races. I had this mare who looked like crow bait but was the fastest thing on four feet. I'd dust her up, put a packsaddle on her, then ride into a town, where Joel'd already be pickin' out the sports. We'd get to talkin' racing and I'd offer to run my saddle horse against anything they could put up. We'd get to arguin' and I'd pretend to get mad and say, hell, I'd bet my old packhorse'd beat their best horse. They'd see the mare and bet their shirts. And then I'd run the mare and take their money. Sometimes we had to leave town on the run, but the Denton mare never let me down.' Bass shook his head. 'That's how come Joel and me left Texas. News about the Denton mare got around and we couldn't get a race anymore. So we signed up to drive this herd up the Chisholm Trail to Dodge. I lost the mare on the way; damn Kiowa shot her out from under me. I was so put out about that, when we got to Dodge we kept right on goin' with the herd. Sold it in Ogallala for eight thousand and kept on, until we got here. Joel and me put the eight thousand into a rich claim. Only it was salted and we sold her for two hundred dollars. Then it turned out the claim wasn't salted after all and the fellow we sold it to sold it for fifty thousand dollars. That's the kind of luck I been havin' and if things don't get better soon, I'm gonna go back to Indiana and get me a job as a hired hand. Well, here we are.'

They had reached a cabin that was not more than twelve by fifteen in size. There was an oil lamp burning inside and as they came up, a man came out with a shotgun in his hands.

'Lon,' said Bass, 'this is Mr. Rawlins. He's buyin' our extra horse.'

'We broke again?' asked Lon.

'We had a bad run of cards,' said Bass, quite cheerfully. 'Fact is, Mr. Rawlins won some of our money. That's why he's paying two hundred for the horse.'

'Two hundred! Why, that plug ain't worth—'

'I know it isn't,' said Rawlins, 'but I need a horse.'

Bass led the way to a corral behind the cabin and brought out a horse by the halter. In the semi-light of the moon, Rawlins could see that the horse was not what he was accustomed to riding, but he had not expected a horse of the caliber of the Denton mare.

He looked the animal over and saw that it was a sound gelding.

'Throw on a saddle and we've got a deal,' he told Bass.

'Wasn't nothin' said about a saddle,' cried Bass. 'The two hundred's for the horse alone.'

Rawlins drew the Navy Colt and pointed it at Sam Bass's midsection. 'When you deal with a thief you expect to be robbed, and I didn't mind up to a point. I was going to pay you the two hundred, then take back the hundred you owe me from the stagecoach robbery. I'll give you one more chance. I'll *give* you the two hundred and you can keep it all—but you're throwing in a saddle.'

Sam Bass thought for a moment, then nodded. 'It's a deal. Lon, throw Bill Clark's saddle on the horse. No—better make it Jim Berry's. I can lick him.'

Lon picked out a saddle from the top rail of the corral and put it on the gelding. Rawlins meanwhile counted out two hundred dollars and gave it to Sam Bass. But he continued to hold the Colt in his hand. Bass did not seem to mind.

He said. 'You want a bill of sale?'

'Would it be any good?'

'It'd be fine—as long as you don't go to Texas.'

'I think I'll let the bill of sale go. I'm not going to Texas. At least I don't think I am.'

Rawlins mounted the horse and gave Sam Bass a short salute with his unemcumbered hand. Then he rode off, putting the horse into a quick trot and bending low in the saddle. It was only when he neared the lighted street of Deadwood that he put away the Navy Colt.

In Deadwood, he took the horse to a livery stable, paid for a night's stalling, then left the livery stable and found a mercantile store still open.

He bought forty dollars' worth of supplies and equipment and, carrying the burlap sack in which the purchases were stowed, he walked back to the hotel.

In the room, a miner was already sprawled on the bed and another was in the act of undressing.

'What the hell,' the second one muttered.

'He was here this afternoon,' said the man on the bed.

'There'll probably be one more later,' said Rawlins. 'The hotel's short of beds. I'll bunk down on the floor.'

'Damn right you will,' growled the second miner.

CHAPTER TWELVE

Rawlins slept very little. The two miners snored lustily, sometimes only one at a time, sometimes together. The smell of their bodies made Rawlins' stomach queasy, but he endured it until three-thirty in the morning, when he got up, noting that Higgins had not yet come into the room. He got his burlap sack and the bag he had come to Deadwood with and left the room quietly.

The night clerk was not behind the desk, but was standing in the open doorway with two or three other men, watching a troop of cavalry ride by. Rawlins deposited his valise and burlap sack on the floor and joined the group by the door.

One of the men said, 'It's true about Custer.'

'He got beat?' asked Rawlins.

'He's dead—him and the whole Seventh Cavalry.'

The cavalry troop on the street came to a halt and the men in the hotel doorway poured out onto the wooden sidewalk. Rawlins went past them and accosted a trooper with yellow sergeant's chevrons.

'Is it true about Custer?' he asked.

The sergeant nodded. 'Never thought they'd get Old Yellow Hair.'

'The entire Seventh's been wiped out?' cried Rawlins.

'That's what they said. Two fellas came in last night, then two more just before we got into the saddle. They're from Terry's outfit. Claim they found Custer and every single man of the Seventh dead on the Little Big Horn. There's thirty thousand Sioux comin' this way . . .'

'Here—to Deadwood?'

'Terry got licked hisself, and Gibbon and Sully got themselves a whippin' like—'

'Sergeant,' shouted an officer a short distance away, 'keep your mouth shut!'

A second officer rode down the line of cavalrymen, from the head of the column. He talked for a moment to the officer who had admonished the sergeant, then the order was given for the troopers to dismount, but maintain ranks.

The sidewalks were filling up by now, but it was a silent crowd that watched the soldiers. Rawlins went back into the hotel, got his bag and burlap sack and walked to the livery stable. The night man stood outside the stable, watching the soldiers.

'These bluecoats gonna protect Deadwood?' he asked. 'Hell, there ain't more'n sixty-seventy of 'em. All they're gonna do is get the whole town massacred.'

'Not me,' said Rawlins. 'I'm leaving now.'

'You ain't the only one,' the livery man said. 'Half the town will be headin' south by noon. Those that won't be goin' east, to Pierre.'

'I left Pierre two days ago,' said Rawlins. 'There aren't enough soldiers there to protect the fort—not against any sizable number of Sioux.'

In the light of the livery stable, his horse looked even worse than it had when Rawlins had bought it. He saddled it, however, fastened the burlap sack and valise onto the pommel, one on each side, and mounted the animal.

He rode out of the stable, past the cavalrymen, and headed south, toward the cabin occupied by Sam Bass and his friends. As he approached he slowed the horse to a careful walk and stopped altogether a hundred feet away. He dismounted and looked at the little cabin, which was well lighted by moonlight. After a moment he exclaimed. The cabin door stood wide open, and he saw that the corral behind the cabin was empty.

Inside the cabin, refuse was scattered about the earthen floor, but there were no occupants. Collins, Bass and the man Rawlins believed was John Bender were gone.

He remounted and started back toward Deadwood, but had gone less than fifty feet when he wheeled the horse around and sent it down the road at a good trot.

It was approximately ten miles to the spot where the stagecoach had been held up less than twenty-four hours ago, and dawn was breaking over the eastern hills when Rawlins estimated that he had traveled the distance.

He identified landmarks ahead and slackened his pace, then pulled the horse off the rutted stagecoach and wagon trail into a growth of stunted pine trees. He dismounted and moved a short distance away, listening. He heard nothing, nothing but the silence of the ages.

He waited. The dawn became daylight and soon it was five-thirty, then six o'clock, when he heard at last the sound of a fast approaching vehicle.

He examined the Navy gun, put it back under his belt and mounted his horse. He moved out toward the road, but remained concealed in a small clump of trees.

The noise of the approaching vehicle became louder and he heard the shouting of the stagecoach driver as he brought his team of four up to the top of the ridge and started downhill. Rawlins kept his eyes on the woods, across the trail. He expected any moment that the road agents would burst out. But the stagecoach came and went past him and no outlaws appeared.

Chagrined, Rawlins left the woods and followed the stagecoach, riding at a distance of several hundred feet. He followed for two miles, then gave up; the road agents had not made their appearance.

The eastbound stage was scheduled to leave Deadwood at six o'clock. It should be coming along in another hour or so. Rawlins rode back to his sheltered spot just before the ridge of the hills. He tied his horse to a sapling and sat down on the ground nearby, his back against a tree.

Yes, the more he thought of it, the surer he felt. The road agents hoped to make a final cleanup. They would expect that the eastbound passengers would have more money than the westbound. And there might be gold dust sent east.

He waited for almost an hour before remounting his horse. Before he could move out, he heard the clatter of metal, the clop-clop of horses' hoofs. He rode quickly into the fringe of trees overlooking the highway.

Four cavalrymen were coming toward him along the road. Behind them was the stagecoach and behind the stagecoach another four soldiers. A cavalry escort had been provided. There would be no holdup of this stagecoach.

Frusrated, as no doubt were the road agents, Rawlins watched the cavalcade riding past his hideout. Lily Lane was on that stage, as was, probably, Marmaduke Higgins.

There was nothing he could do except follow the stage all the way to Pierre, and board a downriver boat to make the slow trip to Omaha, where he could take the Union Pacific west, to Ogallala. But he was not even sure that Ogallala was Lily Lane's destination.

Besides, he was more interested in John Bender's route. Bender and his group were mounted and they most certainly would not want to travel east to Fort Pierre. They were more likely to head due south, into Nebraska, where there were no Indian war parties. Well, that was the way Rawlins would travel. He was prepared for it and sooner or later, he would cut their trail. They had a few hours start on him, but he could travel longer and faster than they could. He had the incentive.

Rawlins rode south and west, and shortly before noon he cut the trail. He got down and studied the tracks of the horses. There were five of them, he decided. The number was right: Sam Bass, Joel Collins, Jim Berry, Lon—and Bill Clark, christened John Bender. He picked up earth and sifted it through his fingers. The trail was several hours old.

He followed the trail of the five riders. He followed it at a fast pace until his horse began to heave, when he stopped and gave the horse a ten minute rest period, permitting him to graze. But the horse refused—he was too far gone.

Rawlins examined the horse and cursed himself for having bought it. It was as poor an animal as he had ever seen, well below the standard of the outlaws' mounts. Well, handling a horse was Rawlins' business. He knew how to conserve the strength of a horse, to get the best it was capable of . . . if he did not let his eagerness to reach his quarry force him to crowd the horse beyond its capabilities.

He nursed the horse throughout the afternoon, resting it frequently and moving it at a walk part of the time, trotting only rarely. But by five o'clock, when he stopped to examine carefully the hoofprints of the horses of the outlaws, he realized that the trail was as old as it had been at noon, when he had first picked it up.

He mounted his horse once more and started forward. Inside of a half mile he pulled up. Again he got down and examined the trail. What he had feared had come true. The road agents had split up in three directions. Two horses had turned off, heading southeast, a single horse had continued due south and the tracks of two horses led southwest.

Rawlins was interested only in one of the men—but which trail was Bender's?

He thought for a moment. Sam and Joel Collins were close friends. They had come from Texas and if they were headed back again they would choose to ride together. Therefore one of the two-horse trails obviously belonged to them.

That left Jim Berry, Lon and John Bender. Berry was from Missouri. If the outlaw group was breaking up permanently he would probably be heading in that direction. But in Missouri and Kansas there was danger for John Bender. There was always the chance of being recognized in familiar territory. Rawlins did not believe that Bender would head southeast. Jim Berry's partner therefore would be Lon.

That left the center, the due south trail of the single rider. It could only be John Bender, going it alone, Rawlins decided to follow the lone trail. It was, of course, a wise choice, for if the five outlaws were merely splitting up temporarily, to confuse anyone who might be following them, they would converge again, sooner or later, and it would be logical for the east and west riders to move to the center.

Rawlins rode due south. It was a rough trail and the moon did not come up to help him. He was traveling by dead reckoning, he realized soon, and when the hills began to flatten out somewhat Rawlins knew that he could not count on the due south direction. He had to have a trail to follow.

He got down from his horse, found that there was no trail to see and decided to eat and rest a while. The moon rose grudgingly and he began to see things around him. There was no trail ahead and Rawlins, moving from left to right, bent low to cut the trail of Bender's horse. The ground was hard, rocky in many places, and he cursed himself for letting his eagerness push him beyond the point where he had lost the trail.

He rode back, veering off on a diagonal

109

left, then cutting back to a diagonal right. He spent an hour, traveling slowly, and then, at last, found the single trail again. It did not go directly south, but turned south by southwest.

He tried to follow it by riding bent over, but found that he could not see the faint hoofprints. Finally he climbed down from the saddle and walked, leading his horse. But, again it was too difficult and he decided to rest. Bender would have made camp by now, but being alone, he would not get up too early in the morning. Rawlins knew he himself would be on the move by dawn and so would be able to gain on Bender before the latter broke camp.

He hobbled his horse and rolled himself up in a blanket that he had purchased in Deadwood. He forced himself to try to sleep, but did no more than doze off from time to time. Long before dawn began to break over the eastern rims of hills, he was fully awake.

His horse was fully rested now and Rawlins kept it moving at a good pace, but by the time he had traveled two hours he began to suspect that he had been outwitted. In another hour he was sure of it.

John Bender had not camped during the night. Riding a good horse he had pressed on, stopping only briefly for short rest periods. Rawlins had been at least five or six hours behind when he had first picked up the trail south of Deadwood; he had lost perhaps two hours searching for the trail, later; he had then stopped for eight hours awaiting daylight. Now he was a good fourteen or fifteen hours behind and it would be impossible to make up the difference even if Bender were to camp the coming night. He was a hundred miles ahead, out of the hill country, well into Nebraska.

Rawlins gave up the trail and rode due south at as steady a pace as his horse could travel. He camped for a while that night, ate some food and rested his horse, then climbed back into the saddle and pressed on, as well as he could in the darkness.

In the morning, he saw a shimmering ribbon straight ahead and knew he was in sight of the Union Pacific tracks, which stretched westward across the continent. He reached the railroad in two hours and followed it westward. A train passed him, going west; a long freight train heading east came along, and soon Rawlins saw a town in the distance.

It was called Sidney and consisted of a railroad depot, cattle pens and a dozen buildings, one of which was a saloon. He had a glass of beer and, inquiring if a man of John Bender's description had been seen in the past fifteen hours, was assured that no strangers had come to Sidney in the last few days. He was disconcerted, then, to learn

111

upon inquiry, that Sidney was the most westward town in the state of Nebraska, more than sixty miles west of Ogallala. Rawlins offered to sell his horse to the saloon keeper and was offered ten dollars for it. Angrily, he went to the mercantile store next door and was finally able to sell the animal for twenty-five dollars.

He carried his valise and what remained of the supplies in the burlap sack to the railroad depot, where he learned that an eastbound passenger and freight train would be along in two hours. He bought a ticket to Ogallala. When he had boarded the train, he walked through it from one end to the other, but saw no familiar faces and he settled down to watch the bleak western Nebraska countryside flit by.

After the rails dipped southward for a while, the train rolled into Julesburg, where there was a ten-minute stop. They soon passed through a tiny hamlet, which Rawlins saw by the name on the railroad depot was called Big Springs. He would soon have cause to remember the name.

Twenty minutes later the whistle whoo-hooed and the train began to slacken speed. It came to a halt in Ogallala and Rawlins descended to the busy station platform.

CHAPTER THIRTEEN

Ogallala was a cattle town, a bustling community not too different from some of the Kansas trail towns he had visited in the past few years. The men on the street were mostly cowboys or cattlemen.

The shops and stores were the usual ones, with saloons, of course, predominating. Rawlins picked out the two largest, which seemed to be very much the same size, and entered one, the Ogallala Saloon & Dance Hall. A stage at the rear indicated that the saloon had entertainment. The proprietor told Rawlins that Lily Lane was not expected, but finally conceded that she was expected to open, for three days, at the Trail's End, his leading competitor.

Rawlins went to the Trail's End. He did not have to inquire about Lily Lane. A huge poster decorating the back bar mirror announced her forthcoming appearance. She was billed on the poster as 'The Greatest Entertainer in the U.S.'

Rawlins carried his bags to the Ogallala Hotel, where he signed the register, Charles Rawlins, Chicago, Illinois. He had scarcely finished writing, when he saw a name, three entries above his own.

'Lucy Paxton, Chicago, Illinois.'

'Miss Paxton,' he said to the clerk. 'I believe she's a friend of mine. A very attractive woman, a blonde.'

'The attractive fits,' said the clerk, 'but the blonde, uh-hu. Miss Paxton is a brunette.' His whistled softly. 'A real pip. She come in on the morning westbound.'

'What room is she in?'

The clerk frowned. 'Hey, now, I don't think I should . . .' Rawlins tossed a silver dollar on the counter. 'Uh, Number 3—right next door to your room, Number 4.'

Rawlins carried his luggage to the second floor, passed Number 3 and entered Room 4, which was cramped in size and contained a cot, a chest of drawers, with a pitcher and washbowl on the chest. Hooks inserted into the wall served in place of clothes closet.

He dropped his bag on the bed, the burlap sack on the floor and, stripping to his waist, shaved and washed himself in cold water. He was aware of movement in Room 3, for the separating wall was very thin.

Putting on a clean shirt, he drew a deep breath and left the room. He stopped outside of Room 3, listened a moment, then knocked.

'Yes?' called out a feminine voice.

'The hotel manager,' said Rawlins. 'Could I talk to you a moment?'

'Not now—I'll be down in a few minutes.'

'It's important, Miss Paxton,' insisted Rawlins.

'Oh, very well,' was the reply through the door.

After a moments wait, the door before Rawlins was opened.

She did not recognize him immediately, but then shock jolted her eyes wide open and she gasped, 'The man from Chicago—the streetcar conductor!'

'We had a date in Chicago,' said Rawlins grimly. 'You ran out on me.'

'How—how did you know I was here?' exclaimed the woman who had called herself Molly Johnson in Chicago and registered as Lucy Paxton in Ogallala.

'I didn't,' said Rawlins, 'until I saw your name on the hotel register. I came to Ogallala to meet . . . Lily Lane.'

'Lily Lane! You know her?'

'I met her in Deadwood.' Rawlins regarded the girl steadily. 'You're a friend of Lily's?'

'Of course. She's my *best* friend. We work together sometimes. In fact . . . well, we're beginning work tomorrow, here in Ogallala.'

'You're a singer?' asked Rawlins sharply.

'Not nearly as good as Lily,' was the reply. 'I've only been at it a couple of years and Lily's been a great help to me.'

'The poster in the Trail's End Saloon only gives Lily's name.'

'She's the star. I—I don't get billing when I appear with her. I'm glad enough to be on the same stage with her. On my own . . . like in

Chicago, I don't do very well.'

'You were singing in Chicago?'

'No—I couldn't find work. Then I heard from Lily and she very generously offered to share the stage with me.'

'Where's your brother, now?'

'My brother? What makes you think I've got a brother?'

'Haven't you?'

'Yes, but not many people know that . . .' A tenseness seemed to have come over Lucy Paxton. Her eyes had narrowed to slits. 'You seem to know a lot about me, Mr.—what is it—Ralls?'

'Rawlins, Charles Rawlins. I gave you my name when we first met.'

'I didn't give you mine though,' said Lucy Paxton, tartly.

'No, you said your name was Molly Johnson.'

'It was the first name I could think of.' The tartness increased in her voice. 'You saw fit to follow me to my hotel . . .'

'From which you immediately ran out.'

'What did you expect me to do? You were taking advantage of a—a trivial incident . . .'

'Was that the reason,' said Rawlins, 'or was it because of . . . my name?'

'Rawlins? Is that supposed to mean something? Sounds like an ordinary enough name to me.'

'I had a brother,' said Rawlins. 'He was a

doctor in Labette County, Kansas . . . Dr. Rawlins . . .'

'And you were a streetcar conductor in Chicago,' said Lucy Paxton, with heavy sarcasm. 'I guess there's only one smart one to a family.'

'You never heard of my brother—or Labette County?'

'There are at least a thousand counties in this country I've never heard of, and I've had very little to do with doctors, since I had the whooping cough when I was a child.'

'Was that in Kansas City—in 1863?'

'Mr. Rawlins,' said Lucy Paxton, 'if that *is* your name, you're beginning to annoy me with your innuendos. What the devil are you driving at?'

'That name you first gave me in Chicago—it was a slip, wasn't it? You once knew a girl named Molly Johnson.'

'Maybe I did, it's a common enough name.'

'It's Lily Lane's real name, isn't it?'

'That's where you're wrong. I happen to know that her name is Sadie Fitch. She's from a small town in Missouri, named Rolla, which also happens to be *my* home town. Any more of your cat-and-mouse questions, Mr. Rawlins?'

'Yes, Lily says she had a cousin, a regular giant, about twenty-five. Let's see, what did she say his name was?'

'Clark!' snapped Lucy Paxton. 'Bill Clark.

Now, if you'll excuse me . . .'

She took a quick step backward and slammed the door in Rawlins' face. He thrust out his hand and pushed, but was too late. Lucy Paxton had shot the bolt inside the door.

He knocked.

'Go away!' cried the voice inside the room. 'I've wasted enough time with—with a streetcar conductor!'

Rawlins grimaced at the closed door, hesitated, then turned away and went down to the hotel lobby. He stood there for a moment, then left the lobby and walked to the railroad depot.

He got a telegraph blank and after thinking a moment wrote:

Adam Pleasanton
125 S. Wabash Ave
Chicago, Illinois

Have located subject. Can you get witness from Kansas to make identification.
                                    Charles Rawlins

He read the message over, started to give it to the station agent, then suddenly said, 'Never mind,' and crumpled the telegram into a ball which he thrust into his pocket.

He returned to the hotel, got some note paper and an envelope from the hotel clerk and, leaning on the desk, wrote a two-page letter, which he addressed to Adam Pleasanton at the detective's office address. He bought a stamp from the clerk, affixed it to the envelope and carried the letter to the railroad depot, where the station agent told him that the letter would go out on the evening train. He handed it to the agent, who glanced at the address and gave Rawlins a sharp look.

'That's a very private letter,' said Rawlins. 'That's why I didn't want to mail it at the post office. Mr. Pleasanton, as you probably know, represents the Union Pacific Railroad . . .'

'I know it,' said the agent. 'In fact, I saw him only a year or so ago, when he came through here with the President's special train. Saw his son, Billy, only a couple of months ago. Won't no one know about this letter. I'll give it to the mail clerk myself.'

'Thanks. I appreciate it.'

Rawlins again returned to the hotel. Realizing that he had not eaten a decent meal in almost three days, he went into the dining room and took a table from which he could see into the lobby.

He had an excellent dinner of steak, apple pie and coffee, then left the dining room for the lobby. It was growing dark outside and the town was beginning to liven up. Some cowboys went galloping past the hotel. A few minutes later another group galloped past in the other direction. They let out a few whoops.

At six-thirty, Rawlins approached the hotel clerk. 'Has Miss Lucy Paxton come down yet?'

"She came down coupla hours ago,' was the reply. 'Said she had to go over to the Trail's End and rehearse.'

Rawlins shook his head, annoyed. She had apparently come down while he was on one of his two trips to the station. He went directly to the Trail's End saloon.

There were only twenty-five or thirty people in the big saloon, nothing like the crowd that had jammed the Golden Nugget in Deadwood. Rawlins saw Lucy Paxton at the rear of the saloon. She was talking with a man wearing a striped shirt and a derby hat, who was seated on a piano stool near the stage. Rawlins stopped at the bar, a few feet away. Lucy Paxton had not yet seen him.

'Beer,' he said to the bartender.

'Cost you twenty-five cents,' was the surly retort. 'We don't sell nothin' here less'n two bits.'

'Whiskey's twenty-five cents?'

'The cowboy stuff, yeah. Bonded whiskey's a half dollar.'

'All you need, apparently, to get rich quick are more customers,' said Rawlins.

'We'll get them tomorrow,' promised the

bartender. 'Miss Lily Lane's going to sing here. She's the best in the country and we ought to pack them in.'

'What about the little lady over there?' asked Rawlins. 'She's a very attractive woman . . .'

'She's a kid, a beginner. Heard her practicin' a little while ago. Lily Lane, she ain't.'

'You've heard Lily Lane?'

'I've heard about her. They say she can make you cry.'

'I heard her in Deadwood. She's good, very good. I'd like to hear her—' he gestured toward Lucy Paxton.

'Stick around. The boss is givin' her a tryout. She sings at eight o'clock and if they don't boo her off the stage she'll have another try at ten o'clock, and mebbe at midnight.'

Rawlins sipped some of the beer that had been set before him and was about to turn around when Lucy Paxton came up beside him. 'You're going to make a nuisance of yourself, aren't you?' she asked.

'Why would I do that?' asked Rawlins. 'I had my supper and I stopped in here for a beer. Maybe I'll play some cards.'

'I'm going to sing here at eight o'clock,' said Lucy Paxton. 'I hope you won't be in the audience.'

'Why?'

'If I see you I'll—I'll be nervous and I don't

121

want to be. A lot depends on my being . . . good.'

'All right,' said Rawlins, 'I'll make you a promise. If I am here at eight o'clock, I won't listen. I won't even look at you. How's that?'

She said, evenly, 'Go to hell, Mr. Rawlins!'

She walked away from him, going through the door to the street. Rawlins followed her. When he saw her go into the hotel, he took a stand on the wooden sidewalk, where, with his back to a lamp post, he could watch the hotel door.

At seven-thirty, she came out wearing an evening gown that was almost a replica of the one Lily Lane had worn when she sang at the Golden Nugget in Deadwood. The evening was rather cool and Lucy wore a light shawl over her shoulders.

She saw Rawlins but showed no sign of recognition. He waited until she had disappeared into the Trail's End, then followed. The place now had more patrons but there was still room at the bar, where only two bartenders were working. And there was elbow room at many of the games.

Rawlins watched a faro game for a while, risked a five dollar bet, won and let the ten ride. He won again, picked up the money and began to play seriously. He was almost a hundred dollar winner, when the piano player crashed down on his keys and, standing up, let out a roar.

'For your pleasure, gentlemen, Lucy Paxton, direct from Chicago!'

There was no applause whatever and the pianist sat down again and began to play. Lucy had selected for her first number *Camptown Races*. If anyone aside from Rawlins was listening, he did not show it by applauding when she finished. Rawlins alone clapped and when he kept on one or two men joined in briefly.

Rawlins left the vicinity of the faro game and moved to the bar, not far from where Lucy was on stage. He stood there while she sang one of the more popular songs of the day. This one drew a ripple of applause when she concluded, but Rawlins' clapping was loud and sustained.

Lucy Paxton had not been a success, however, and her face was white and strained when she left the stage. She passed near Rawlins, her eyes averted until she was almost up to him. Then she looked at him. 'Thank you,' she said in a low tone.

'Let me buy you a drink,' he said quickly.

She shook her head, smiling wanly and went on. Rawlins followed her from the saloon to the hotel. He saw her go up the stairs in the hotel and sat down in the lobby. He sat there until ten o'clock, keeping his eyes open with difficulty.

Lucy Paxton did not come downstairs again. Apparently, she felt it was not worthwhile going back to the Trail's End. Rawlins got up, climbed the stairs and went into his own room. He listened at the wall for a moment, but there was no sound from Lucy's room

Rawlins shot the bolt of his door, undressed and went to bed.

CHAPTER FOURTEEN

Earlier, in Deadwood, after the news of Custer's defeat had spread, Joel Collins had remembered a deserted sodbuster's house three miles west of Ogallala, and it had been designated as the meeting place for the road agents. Collins and Sam Bass were the first to reach it, but Jim Berry and Lon Ewing came along late in the afternoon.

Since leaving Deadwood, all of the men had been on short rations. They had traveled long and hard and they were tired—and hungry. Sam Bass and Joel Collins were known in Ogallala and were loath to enter the town. They decided to send Lon Ewing into Ogallala to buy food. Lon had less than four dollars in his pockets. The other road agents emptied their own pockets and learned to their dismay that there was twenty-two dollars in the entire group.

'Looks like we go back into the stagecoach

business,' said Joel Collins sourly.

'I'm through with that chicken-feed stuff,' said Sam Bass.

'You think you're ready for a bank?' asked Collins sarcastically. 'Well, Ogallala's got a bank, a mighty good one, too . . .'

Sam Bass frowned. 'The trouble with banks is you got to hold them up in broad daylight. Ogallala's too busy a town for that—and there's too damn many people with guns. What you need is a small town that ain't very busy, but's got a bank with plenty of cash. Ogallala's got the bank, but it's got too many people in it.'

'A train,' said Jim Berry. 'When I was with Jesse and Frank . . .'

'Hell,' said Joel Collins, 'you never rode with Jesse and Frank and you know it. Keep that stuff for somebody else.'

But Bass held up a detaining hand. 'Wait a minute, Joel, the idea ain't a bad one. It's the way I been thinkin' myself. I been readin' about the trains that Jesse's held up and I think the five of us—if Clark ever shows up—can handle the job.'

'You hold up the Union Pacific,' said Joel Collins, 'you'll have every sheriff in the state after you—and the Pleasanton Detective Agency to boot.'

'I get my hands on a big bankroll,' said Bass, 'I'm headin' straight back to Texas. I'm clean in Texas.'

125

'No, you're not,' retorted Collins. 'There's that business of the cattle we sold in Ogallala that we didn't really own.'

'All right, all right,' said Sam Bass, 'but Texas is a mighty big state . . .' He pointed at Jim Berry. 'You, Jim, what would you do with five thousand dollars?'

'Five thousand dollars!' cried Berry. 'Hell, with that much money I'd go back to Missouri. I'd be a rich man . . .'

'And you, Lon?' asked Bass.

'There ain't that much money, Sam!'

'Jesse's bunch never got less'n twenty-five thousand in a train job,' said Sam Bass.

Joel Collins looked at the eager faces around him and shook his head. 'All right,' he conceded, 'I'm against it, but I'll go along.' He looked darkly at Bass. 'But I'm goin' my own way afterwards.'

That was how Sam Bass became the leader of the newly organized band of train robbers.

Lon Ewing went into Ogallala to buy some food and extra ammunition. Some time later, a lone rider was seen coming from the northeast. As he got nearer, the bandits saw that it was Bill Clark, at last. He was greeted warmly by the other bandits and while he refreshed himself with the first good food he had eaten in several days, Sam Bass outlined the train robbery plan. Clark listened indifferently.

'It's all the same to me,' he said, finally,

126

'stagecoaches or trains. How much you figure my share'll be?'

'Five thousand,' said Bass promptly.

'Five thousand, eh? You guarantee that?'

'If there ain't five thousand,' said Sam Bass, 'I'll split my share with you. If there's more . . .'

'Uh-uh, five thousand's good enough for me. When do we hold up this train?'

'Tomorrow morning. There's usually some California gold on the eastbound trains and I thought we'd stop the one goes through Ogallala around five o'clock. Only we're not going to stop her at Ogallala. Too many people there. Big Spring's ten-twelve miles west of here. There's a railroad depot—'

'On'y the train don't stop at Big Springs,' said Collins. 'Place ain't big enough.'

'She'll stop,' said Sam Bass. 'We'll *make* her stop.'

    ★   ★   ★

Big Springs consisted of a railroad depot, a section house and a half dozen soddies—earth-covered shacks. One frame house stood near the railroad depot and was occupied by the railroad agent.

He had gone to bed early and was already awake when he heard the pounding on his door. He climbed hurriedly into his trousers. When he opened the door, he saw two men

127

standing on the porch and beyond them three men on horses.

'There's a train comin' through here in a half hour,' said one of the men on the porch. 'We want you to stop it.'

'I can't do that,' said the station agent. 'It never stops at Big Springs—not the Limited.'

'She's stopping this morning,' said Sam Bass cheerfully. 'On account of you're going to flag her with your little red lantern . . .'

'Here's a little persuader,' said Bill Clark, producing a huge revolver, 'just to show you we mean business.'

He took a quick step forward and smashed the barrel of the gun along the side of the station agent's face. The man went down like an axed steer and it took ten precious minutes to revive him, during which Sam Bass cursed Clark roundly.

Dawn was breaking when the station agent finally was able to reach the railroad depot under his own power. There, Bass issued his orders and the men began to deploy. When the headlights of the eastbound limited appeared far down the railroad tracks, there were only two men on the station platform—the agent with his lighted red lantern and big Bill Clark, at whom the agent kept looking apprehensively over his shoulder.

The agent stepped down between the railroad tracks and began to wave his lantern

128

back and forth in the prescribed signal. The train whistled in acknowledgment and began to slacken speed as it approached the station at Big Springs, Nebraska.

Before the huge engine wheels ground to a complete stop, Sam Bass grabbed the iron handrail and swung onto the engine platform. At the same time, Lon Ewing appeared from the other side.

'Up with 'em,' roared Sam Bass.

'A holdup!' cried the astonished engineer.

The fireman, caught with a coal scoop in his hands, started to raise the scoop and strike at Sam Bass, Bass sent a bullet whistling past his head. 'That ain't the way we play the game, mister,' he said.

The fireman dropped the scoop and moved closer to his fire box.

'That's more like it,' continued Sam. 'Lon, you think you can keep them here, nice and quiet?'

'They make a move, there'll be a dead fireman and engineer,' said Lon Ewing. He held his revolver carelessly in his right hand as he took a step backward, so that there was sufficient room between him and the engine crew.

Sam Bass swung down from the engine and began running back to the express car where Joel Collins and Jim Berry were banging on the door with their revolvers.

'Open her up,' roared Collins. 'Open her

129

up or we'll dynamite you open!'

A rifle bullet tore through the door from the inside and narrowly missed Joel Collins. Collins fired three times through the door, but moved aside.

Sam Bass moved up. 'You inside, we're buildin' a fire under you. We'll burn up the whole damn train if you don't open her up.'

That produced only silence from inside the express car. 'All right, Jim—Joel, get some wood,' ordered Sam Bass. He called to Bill Clark. 'You, Bill, bring over that there bench. It'll make a fine blaze.'

Clark stowed away his revolver and caught up the big wooden bench that stood outside the depot. He brought it over to the express car and hurled it underneath. Collins and Berry went into the depot itself and soon came out, Collins with two chairs, Berry with an armful of stove wood, some of it split to kindling size.

'Hey,' cried Sam Bass, 'that's all right.'

The combustibles were placed under the express car and a match was soon applied to the kindling wood. While the fire began to blaze up, the conductor at the rear of the train stepped to the ground and fired at the bandits with a small-caliber revolver.

Bass sent two bullets zinging near him and the conductor scrambled for the steps leading into the day coach. They had no more trouble from him.

Flames began to lick at the floor of the express car. Inside, the messenger smelled the smoke and decided that the wisest course was for him to surrender. He opened the side door and threw out a .45 caliber Winchester. Bass, Joel Collins, Jim Berry and Bill Clark poured into the express car.

Herding the messenger ahead of him, Bass went directly toward the iron safe at the front of the express car.

'Open her up!' Bass commanded.

'Can't,' said the messenger. 'I don't know the combination. It's a through safe and she can't be opened until we get to Chicago.'

Joel Collins fired his revolver at the messenger's foot, clipping the edge of his boot toe and going into the floor of the car. 'The next bullet goes through your ankle,' snarled Collins.

'No,' said Bass, 'we ain't cripplin' nobody.'

Collins whirled on Bass. 'You runnin' this goddam circus?'

'I am,' replied Sam Bass calmly, 'and I don't hold with hurtin' nobody.' He added sharply. 'Not if it ain't necessary.'

Collins glowered at him and for a moment it seemed that he would challenge Bass, but he moved aside. 'All right, you're the boss.'

Bass turned back to the express messenger. 'You sure enough can't open that there safe?'

The express messenger could not quite conceal a gleam of triumph. Sam Bass saw it

131

and knew that his apparent reluctance to shed blood had cost him. There was an ax standing beside the door of the safe.

He caught it up and smashed the head of the ax against the dial on the safe. The axhead bounced off the tempered steel of the dial, hit the iron safe door, but did not even gouge it.

Bass swung again. He missed the dial this time and the ax ricocheted off the door of the safe and struck a stack of small wooden boxes beside the safe. The top box went hurtling to the floor, broke—and spilled out a shower of bright yellow coins.

'Gold!' cried Sam Bass, exultantly. 'We've struck pay dirt!'

He whisked a sack out from under his coat, dropped to his hands and knees and began to scoop up the gold and dump it into the sack. Bill Clark came forward and picked up both of the remaining wooden boxes. Their weight indicated that they, too, were full of gold coins.

That completed the holdup.

The train robbers gathered outside the express car and Sam, firing into the air, brought Lon Ewing down from the engine cab.

In a shallow coulee two miles north of Big Springs, Joel Collins, who was in the lead, pulled up his horse. 'This is as good a place as any to divvy up,' he announced.

Sam Bass shook his head. 'We ought to put

some distance between us and Big Springs.'

'There's nobody in Big Springs to chase us,' said Joel Collins. 'I want my cut . . . now!'

Sam Bass saw the greed in the eyes of the other outlaws and dismounted. The two untouched boxes were dumped on the ground and Sam took the sack containing the gold coins that he had gathered up from the broken box in the express car.

He got down on his knees and began counting twenty-dollar gold pieces. He made a small pile of two-hundred and fifty coins, counted out two-hundred and fifty coins into another stack, then continued with a third stack. When he concluded the third stack he looked up at big Bill Clark.

'What did I promise you, Bill?'

'Five thousand . . .'

Sam Bass pushed one of the piles of coins toward the big man. 'There she is, five thousand dollars!'

'Whoa—now just a damn minute!' cried Jim Berry. 'There's more'n five thousand apiece in those boxes.'

Sam Bass rocked back on his heels. His right hand was very close to his revolver. 'Five thousand apiece is what I promised you—and five thousand is what you get. Anybody got any objection?'

Joel Collins stooped over and picked up one of the unopened boxes of coins. His right hand fell to his side. 'The leader always get a bigger cut,' he said grimly. 'Anybody say I ain't the leader anymore?'

Bass looked up at Collins thoughtfully. 'We been friends a long time, Joel . . .'

'We're not friends anymore,' said Collins. 'I'm pullin' out now.' He looked around. 'Lon, you goin' with me, like you said you would?'

Lon Ewing gathered up one of the piles of five thousand gold coins. 'I'm with you, Joel.'

He went to his horse. Collins backed to his own mount, waited for Sam Bass to challenge him again, but when Bass did not, Collins mounted his horse.

Bass exhaled heavily. 'Now, let's get on with this, Jim?'

Berry hesitated, then shrugged suddenly. 'I'll ride with you, Sam.'

He dropped to his knees and began to pick up his money.

Bass looked again at the giant. 'Any complaints, Clark?'

'Hell,' said the big man, 'how much whiskey can a man drink? Five thousand'll hold me for quite a spell.' His tongue came out and licked his lips. 'On'y I think I'll ride alone, for a spell.'

'Suits me,' said Sam Bass.

CHAPTER FIFTEEN

It was eight-thirty when Rawlins descended to the hotel lobby and found it filled with a chattering group of townspeople. The talk caught his attention and he clapped a man on the shoulder.

'What kind of holdup?'

The man gave Rawlins an impatient look over his shoulder. 'Union Pacific!'

'Where?' exclaimed Rawlins. The man in front of him paid no attention and Rawlins had to catch the arm of another man.

'Where was the holdup—and when?'

'Big Springs,' was the reply. 'Just come over the telegraph. Early this morning . . .'

Then he heard, 'Jesse James, sure's shootin'. He never goes after a train unless it's got gold on it.'

'How much?' cried Rawlins.

'Sixty thousand.'

Rawlins whistled softly. He stepped to the door, hesitated, then walked swiftly to the Union Pacific depot.

The station agent was on duty. It was he, in fact, who had gotten the news of the holdup on the telegraph key. 'Heard about the holdup at Big Springs?' he asked as he saw Rawlins.

'I heard about it at the hotel. How many

men were there in the gang?'

'Five, according to what I got on the wire. All of them masked, but what the hell, it had to be old Jesse again.'

'Not necessarily,' said Rawlins.

'Who else is got the nerve?'

'I want to send a telegram,' said Rawlins. 'A confidential telegram.'

The agent looked at him sharply. 'To—Adam Pleasanton?'

'Yes.'

'I thought so. You work for him, don't you?'

Rawlins did not reply. He caught up a pencil, wrote Pleasanton's name and office address, then added:

Have important information about holdup at Big Springs. Please advise.

Rawlins

The agent read the telegram.

'You talk to Sheriff Whitmore?' he asked. 'He's already sent out a posse and's gettin' another ready.'

'I don't work for the sheriff,' said Rawlins. 'Send this at once. It's urgent.'

'I can imagine.' The agent went immediately to his key and began clicking it. When he finished he looked at Rawlins. 'You can't possibly get an answer inside of an hour. I'll let you know soon's it comes. You're at the hotel, aren't you?'

'Yes, I'll wait there.'

The station agent nodded and Rawlins walked back to the hotel. There were already clumps of men on the streets and sidewalks, all discussing the holdup at Big Springs. Rawlins stopped at one of the groups and got some new details. The five bandits, he learned, had gone to the station agent's home while it was still dark, had forced him to accompany them to the depot and there to signal the train to stop. The agent had resisted and had been savagely clubbed with a revolver by a man who, from his size, could only have been Cole Younger. Another man, however, was obviously the leader and that had to be Jesse James. A third man seemed to have authority also and that, according to talk, must have been Frank James, Jesse's brother.

Sixty thousand dollars. If the money was divided evenly, that was twelve thousand apiece for each of the five men. John Bender could travel a long way with twelve thousand dollars. Sam Bass, if he ran true to form, would gamble away his twelve thousand before he ever reached Texas again. He could continue his outlaw career there, remembering that he had once struck it really big. He would always be trying to top that figure.

Rawlins left the group and walked on to the

hotel. The lobby had emptied, but the clerk immediately began speaking to Rawlins about the holdup.

Rawlins sat down in the chair he had occupied the evening before. 'Has Miss Paxton come down for breakfast yet?' he asked.

'She's in now,' said the clerk, pointing to the dining room.

In the dining room, there were people at only two tables. Lucy Paxton was alone at one of them. Rawlins went up to her.

'Have you heard about the train robbery?' he asked.

She nodded. 'The clerk insisted on telling me. I'm afraid I'm not much interested in train holdups.'

'You might be in this one,' Rawlins said, 'if you knew who was in on the job?'

'Jesse James,' said Lucy. 'I heard all about it.'

'Uh-uh, it wasn't Jesse, this time. One of them's an old townsman of yours—Bill Clark.'

'Bill Clark?'

'Of Rolla, Missouri. Your friend Lily Lane's cousin.'

'What are you talking about? You said last night that he was in Deadwood, Dakota Territory.'

'I said he *was* there. As a matter of fact, that's why I'm in Nebraska. Clark pulled out of Deadwood with his friends and I followed them here. Only I lost their trail.'

Rawlins became aware that Lucy was suddenly looking beyond him and turned. A heavyset man of about forty was bearing down on him. He wore black-striped trousers, boots and a flannel shirt on which was a badge, lettered 'Sheriff.'

'Mr. Rawlins,' he said, 'I'm Sheriff Whitmore. I'd like to have a word with you . . . alone . . .'

'Of course.' Rawlins nodded to Lucy. 'Excuse me.'

The sheriff touched his hat brim. 'Ma'am,' then followed Rawlins out of the dining room. When they entered the lobby, Rawlins saw the Union Pacific agent standing just inside the door.

The agent shook his head. 'Sorry, Mr. Rawlins, I live in this town.'

'He was only doing his job,' said the sheriff. 'I've a right to see copies of all telegrams sent. Will you walk over to my office and have a little talk?'

'If I say no?'

'We'll still go to my office,' said the sheriff. 'Only I'll be talking to you through the bars, in that case.'

There was no way out and Rawlins accompanied the sheriff to the most substantially-built building in Ogallala, a one-story brick structure, which had the sheriff's office in front and the jail in the rear.

A deputy was examining the rifles on an unlocked gun rack in the office. He barely glanced up as Rawlins came in.

The sheriff wasted little time. 'Your telegram said you had important information about the Big Springs holdup.'

'Sheriff,' said Rawlins, 'as you probably suspect after having read the telegram, I work for Adam Pleasanton. With all due respect, I'd rather not answer your questions until after I hear from Mr. Pleasanton.' He added quickly, 'Which should be inside of an hour.'

'I can't wait an hour,' said the sheriff. 'I've got a second posse ready to go right now and I'd like to go with them. If your information can help us . . .'

'I can't help you find the robbers,' said Rawlins. 'I haven't the slightest idea of which direction they went. The information I have is—well, it's only a guess.'

'I know Adam Pleasanton,' said the sheriff. 'Any man of his has got to have facts, not just guesses.'

'It's more than a guess,' said Rawlins. 'It's *almost* a certainty. I know the men who pulled the job.'

The sheriff stared at Rawlins, as his face reddened. 'And *that* you want to hold back?' His face twisted angrily. 'Dammit, that's more important than any direction you can give me. Who are the men?'

140

'You won't know the names.'

'The hell I won't. I know every damn thief and robber in this territory. I've been a lawman for eleven years, ever since the war.'

'Did you ever hear of a man named Joel Collins? Sam Bass?'

'No, but . . .'

'They were in Ogallala some months ago. They sold a herd here, that they didn't own.'

'Wait—I remember that case. Nobody knew the herd wasn't their'n until they was long gone.'

'Then you don't remember the men? You couldn't pick them out of a small crowd?'

'You can?'

Rawlins nodded. 'And the three men with them, a man called Lon, one named Jim Berry, who claims he rode with Jesse James during the war . . . and the fifth man uses the name of Bill Clark.'

'I never heard of *any* of them.'

'They were two-bit stage coach robbers in Deadwood,' said Rawlins. 'As a matter of fact, they held up a stagecoach that I was riding on and I had some trouble with them in town. There wasn't anything I could do about it, but, I followed them from Deadwood.'

'Why? Adam Pleasanton chasin' small-time crooks these days?'

'I'm interested in one of the men—on another matter entirely!'

141

'Which one?'

'The man who calls himself Clark. He's about the biggest man you've ever seen. A murderer, from Kansas.'

'I got a *dodger* on him?'

'Probably—under his real name.'

'What's that?'

'Bender. John Bender.'

The sheriff frowned for a moment, then exclaimed, 'The man who killed all those people with an ax? Hell, there was a whole family mixed in that. They axed twenty-some people.'

'One of them was my brother!'

'Mister,' said the sheriff, 'I'll make a deal with you. Help me catch this bunch and I'll turn Bender over to you. You can take him back to Kansas, or you can . . . well, you can do what you want with him.'

The deputy across the room, said laconically: 'Train's in.'

Rawlins heard it then, the tolling of a train bell. 'Someone's on that train I want to see.'

The sheriff started to scowl. 'I'll walk over to the depot with you. Then we'll start out after the train robbers, hey?'

'All right,' agreed Rawlins.

The train had already pulled into the station and passengers were descending when the sheriff and Rawlins arrived. In the vanguard were Marmaduke Higgins and Lily Lane; Higgins was carrying his own valise, as

142

well as two bags that obviously belonged to Lily, who herself carried a rather heavy box.

'Rawlins!' cried Higgins. 'You're the last man in the world I expected to see here.'

He deposited the luggage on the edge of the platform, grabbed Rawlins' hand and pounded his shoulder. Rawlins' eyes were on Lily Lane. She was smiling warmly.

'Still picking fights, Mr. Rawlins?'

'Only with women,' retorted Rawlins, 'as you'll be told only too soon.' He paused. 'By Lucy Paxton.'

'Oh, no!' wailed Lily.

'I just left her at the hotel. I guess I spoiled her breakfast for her.' He turned to Higgins. 'Our Deadwood friends have really done it. That Big Springs holdup this morning—'

'We heard about that on the train,' said Higgins, 'but the report was that it was Jesse . . .' he inhaled sharply. 'Surely, you're not suggesting.'

'Sam Bass and company. They've hit the big time.'

'Mr. Rawlins,' called the sheriff, from a short distance away. 'Would you mind?'

The sheriff had stopped a few feet away, where he was talking to a veritable giant of a man.

'Excuse me a minute,' said Rawlins. He left Higgins and Lily and walked over to the sheriff. He was sure that the big man was studying him closely.

'Mr. Rawlins,' said the sheriff, 'shake hands with Mr. William Pleasanton.'

The big man thrust out a huge hand and gripped Rawlins' hand in a powerful grip. 'I know about you, Mr. Rawlins, but I didn't think I'd meet you so soon.'

'Mr. Pleasanton was on his way to Denver, when he got news of the holdup,' said the sheriff.

Pleasanton nodded. 'The sheriff tells me that you may know the people did the job. I think it'd be a good idea if we got after them, right away.'

Rawlins sent a quick look toward Higgins and Lily Lane, who seemed to be waiting for him to return to them. 'Just a moment.' He stepped quickly across to Higgins and Lily.

'I'm sorry,' he said, 'but I've got to go now.' He dropped his voice to a whisper as he leaned closer to Lily. 'I'm afraid your cousin Bill Clark's in trouble.'

She exclaimed in annoyance. 'You're still harping on that!'

Marmaduke Higgins said, 'My luck changed on the River Queen. I won eight hundred dollars between Fort Pierre and Omaha.'

'Don't lose it in Ogallala,' said Rawlins.

CHAPTER SIXTEEN

There were eight men in the posse—the sheriff, Rawlins, huge Billy Pleasanton and five cowboys who had been stranded in Ogallala, having spent their trail pay. The sheriff had promised them five dollars a day.

They reached the little hamlet of Big Springs, riding at a canter all the way from Ogallala. The sheriff led the way to the railroad depot, where a crowd of citizens had gathered. The station agent, they were told by the townsmen, was at his home nearby. He had been badly beaten with a gun.

The posse moved quickly to the station agent's house, where the sheriff, Billy Pleasanton and Rawlins got down from their horses. They were met at the doorway by the station agent's wife, who led them into the bedroom.

The agent lay in bed, a huge blood-stained bandage almost concealing his features. 'It was the big fella hit me,' he told the sheriff weakly. 'Must have been Cole Younger. They say he's big and mean . . .'

Rawlins said, 'Did any of them talk like Texans?'

'Yeah, sure, two of 'em,' said the agent.

'Did you gather that either of them was the leader?'

145

The man hesitated. 'Yeah, but come to think of it, they musta been disguisin' their voices, on account of—well, Jesse James's from Missouri, ain't he?' He hesitated again. 'The youngest one of the bunch acted like he was bossin' the job.'

'Sam Bass,' said Rawlins.

'Until today,' said Billy Pleasanton, 'I never heard of Sam Bass, but from the sound of this it's a name we're going to hear a lot of.' Then he added, thoughtfully, 'Unless we get him in the next few days.'

'If we don't get him I'll turn in my badge,' promised the sheriff.

They left the house and were mounting their horses, when they became aware of a man a block away, galloping toward them. The sheriff waited a moment, then suddenly spurred his horse to meet the approaching horseman. The others followed at a slower pace.

The approaching rider was a member of the posse that had taken the field earlier in the day. His report was disconcerting.

'We found the boxes the coin was in. Apparently they stopped to divvy up.'

'They're going to split!' exclaimed Rawlins.

'They already have,' said the rider. 'Three ways. There were ten of us, so Moser divided the posse into three chunks and sent me to report to you.'

The sheriff nodded. 'Counting you, there's

146

nine of us. We'll split into three bunches of three, so there'll be six to two in two of the posses and six to one in the other. That ought to be enough to handle them.'

One of the five cowboys rode up from the group. 'Sheriff,' he said, 'we just heard that the fellas did this job was from Texas.'

'So what? There's riffraff in Texas, too.'

The cowboy shook his head. 'Me'n the boys been talkin'. We wouldn't feel right goin' after Texas fellas.'

'Only two of them are Texans,' snapped the sheriff. 'The others are from Missouri.'

'If it's just the same to you, then, we'll go after the Missouri boys. Some of them fought with us in the war, but it ain't like goin' after kinfolk, so to speak.'

'All right, I'll go after the Texas fellows. Mr. Pleasanton, suppose you take this fine bunch of Texas fellas and go chase the Missouri boys.'

The spokesman for the cowboys was not satisfied with that. 'Tell you the truth, sheriff, we just found out that this here fella—well, we just learned he is the son of the fella's got the Pleasanton Detective Agency and down in Texas we don't feel so good about the Pleasanton Detective Agency.'

Billy Pleasanton said, 'It happens that my father and I both agree with General Phil Sheridan. You know what he said: "If I owned Texas and Hell I'd rent out Texas and

147

live in Hell!" I'll ride with no posse that has Texas men in it. Sheriff, if it's all the same with you I'll ride back to Ogallala.'

'Give my regards to your father,' the sheriff said scornfully.

Rawlins thought for a moment that the detective was going to go for the sheriff, but Pleasanton held himself in very well. He looked at Sheriff Whitmore for a long moment, then said, 'Mr. Rawlins, will you ride with me?'

'He goes with me,' snarled the sheriff. 'He's the only man can identify this crowd.'

'Each one of those men is loaded with twenty-dollar gold coins,' said Billy Pleasanton. 'Do you need more identification than that?' Then he added, 'May I remind you, Sheriff, that the railroad employs our agency on a yearly retainer?'

'The railroad didn't elect me,' snapped the sheriff. 'In fact, they backed the man I beat. I figger I don't owe the railroad a damn thing.'

'I'll tell them that—in my report,' said the big detective. He nodded again to the sheriff and looked inquiringly at Rawlins.

'Mr. Pleasanton,' Rawlins said, 'your father knows how long I've been after John Bender. This is the last chance I have to catch up with him and—'

'All right,' said Pleasanton. 'You've made your choice.'

He turned his horse, put it to a trot, then

into a gallop. The sheriff watched him go. 'That horse will founder before he gets half way to Ogallala.' Then he caught sight of the five cowboys watching him. 'You're fired, the bunch of you.'

'We want our pay,' said one of the Texas men.

The sheriff could restrain himself no longer. Although he wound up paying each man five dollars, he gave them a blistering verbal sendoff as they rode off.

'I get back to Ogallala and I find one of them still there, he'll pay a visit to the jail,' he told Rawlins.

Rawlins made no comment and after a moment or two he and the sheriff and the remaining posse man rode off. The trail was due north for about two miles, then turned eastward. They went another mile or so in a small wooded coulee, when they came upon the remnants of a wooden box that the outlaws had broken. They dismounted and the sheriff looked around, but there was nothing else and they remounted.

Within a hundred yards, the trail split in three. The hoofprints of two horses led due east, those of another pointed north, the last two went east by south.

'This'll be Bass and Collins,' said the sheriff. 'Come on, Rawlins.'

'No,' said Rawlins, 'I'm going after John Bender.'

'The hell you will,' said the sheriff. He whipped out his revolver and thrust it at Rawlins. 'I need you to identify these boys. Simpson, take his gun!'

The third posse member hesitated, but he apparently knew the sheriff well. He got down from his horse, bent low to be out of the range of fire and moved up to Rawlins, reaching under his coat to draw the Navy Colt from Rawlins' belt.

'I should have stayed with Billy Pleasanton,' said Rawlins.

'There's three fellows already after Bender,' said the sheriff. 'And three after the Missouri fellas. We'll go after the Texas lads—they've probably got the biggest part of the split—and they're the leaders. Simpson, you ride ahead, then you, Rawlins, and I'll bring up the rear.'

The soil was sandy and the tracks of the fugitives and the three posse members who were already on their trail were easy to follow.

Simpson led the way at a swift canter, and now and then even put his horse into a short gallop. They went perhaps five miles and saw the railroad tracks ahead. The trail went across them and continued due south. But two miles below the Union Pacific rails, they came upon a small, discouraged group of horsemen waiting for the sheriff and his aides. 'They've split up again,' one of them said to the sheriff. He pointed diagonally with his left hand to the southeast. 'One of them's gone that way. The other . . .' He pointed with his right hand to south-west.

The sheriff went into a sudden rage. 'How much time have you lost here? An hour?'

'Wasn't mor'n a half hour,' was the reply. 'We was tryin' to decide which one'd go it alone.'

'Damn you for a bunch of chicken-livered cowards,' snarled the sheriff. 'All right, there's six of us now. Do you think three to one is good enough odds for you?'

'It's all right with me,' said one of the posse.

'Then get going—the three of you.' He pointed east. 'Rawlins, you and Simpson— we'll take the right trail. And I hope to hell it's Sam Bass!'

The three men followed the single trail leading to the southwest. It was still fairly easy to follow, but it was a single trail now, not a group of riders, and the posse could not follow it at a swift pace.

After a half hour on the trail, Simpson pulled up his horse and waited for Rawlins and the sheriff to come up.

'I've been thinkin', sheriff. These Texas boys know horses better'n anything else. They're riding by the time they're three years old . . .'

The sheriff made an impatient gesture. 'Get on with it, man!'

'The south fork of the Platte's up ahead, 'bout eight miles,' Simpson went on. 'I happen to know it's pretty full and I doubt if our boy's goin' to try to swim it with a tired horse. He's goin' to be lookin' for a ford and there's one ten-twelve miles up river. Lem Goss's got a little store there and I think our friend's goin' to grub up and try to make hisself a horse trade. I say, we strike across country to Goss's place. We'll cut off six-eight miles and maybe catch up to him there.'

The sheriff frowned a moment. 'I've been by Goss's place and you may have somethin' there, Simpson. I'm willing to give it a try.'

The trio left the trail of the outlaw's tracks and headed across country, to the southwest. They drove their horses as hard as they could and Rawlins doubted whether his own mount could sustain the pace, after the grueling trip it had already made, but the other horses were in no better condition and the sheriff was the first to pull up his horse to an easier pace.

He pressed on impatiently even then, complaining continually that Rawlins was holding him back. When Rawlins thought that his horse would founder completely they saw at last the little cluster of buildings that belonged to Goss.

CHAPTER SEVENTEEN

There were no horses outside the little trading post, but a single animal was in the corral nearby. A buckboard stood outside a small blacksmith shop at the rear of the store. No one was inside the blacksmith shop, however, and in fact there was no sign of human life at all.

The sheriff pulled up his horse. 'He's been here and gone.'

'I don't see Lem,' said Simpson. 'He's usually outside, waitin' for you to come up.'

The sheriff drew up his rifle and rode forward.

Rawlins said: 'Don't you think it's time to give me back my gun?'

The sheriff started to draw Rawlins' Navy Colt from under his belt, then shook his head. 'Later.'

Simpson seemed reluctant to approach the buildings. 'I don't like the look of this,' he said.

'Neither do I,' retorted the sheriff, 'but there ain't only one man and damned if . . .'

The front door of the store was slammed open and a man stepped out, with a double-barreled shotgun in his hands. It was Bill Clark. The sheriff whipped his Winchester around and sent a quick shot in

153

Clark's direction. It was the last thing the sheriff did on this earth . . . except topple from his saddle, as the blast from Clark's shotgun caught him full in the face and chest.

Rawlins, a few feet to the left and the rear of the sheriff, reacted instinctively. He kneed his tired horse savagely and sent it forward, toward the man in front of the store. Before the animal reached Clark, Rawlins sprang from the saddle. He landed heavily and threw himself forward, at full length.

It saved his life, for Clark fired the second barrel of his shotgun and Rawlins felt the blast go over him. He scrambled to his feet and lunged for the big man.

Clark poked the barrel of the shotgun at Rawlins. Rawlins knocked it aside, hurting his left hand, and struck the giant a savage blow with his right.

Clark let out a roar and hurled the shotgun away. 'Looks like we're gonna have that fight after all!' he said. He threw out his hands and sprang for Rawlins.

With his left hand he struck at Rawlins, gripping his elbow. He jerked Rawlins to him and threw his other arm about him. Rawlins flailed at the giant's face with both hands. They were hard blows, but they seemed to have no effect on Clark. The big man's tremendous arms tightened about Rawlins and forced the air from his lungs.

A roaring began to fill Rawlins' ears. He

154

continued to smash his fists into Clark's face, but knew it would be all over for him in a minute or two.

He was not aware that, behind him, Simpson had dismounted and was trying to get a shot at Clark with his revolver. But Rawlins' back was to him and he was afraid the bullet would hit Rawlins instead. He danced up close, jumped high to get at Clark and finally smashed down with the barrel of his gun.

The blow caught Clark high on the forehead and apparently hurt him, for the big man let out a roar. With one violent move he whirled Rawlins aside and, leaping forward, smashed Simpson with his fist. Simpson turned a complete somersault, his revolver flying from his hand. Simpson kicked once or twice, then lay still.

Rawlins had gone down to his knees and was struggling to his feet as the giant turned on him once more. He tried to dodge, but Clark lashed out with a furious kick that caught Rawlins high on the shoulder and sent him to the ground. Clark came forward and kicked Rawlins in the ribs.

Pain in the rib cage brought Rawlins back to full consciousness. He rolled over completely, came up on his knees and dove for the big man as he came at him again. Locking his arms about Clark's knees, Rawlins heaved and upset him.

That was Rawlins' chance. He scrambled to his feet and looked quickly for a weapon. The dead sheriff lay thirty feet away; Simpson was closer, but his gun was nowhere in sight. Rawlins ran toward the sheriff, but heard Clark behind him bellowing. At the last instant he knew he would be too late and gave up the attempt to get the sheriff's Winchester. He sprang aside instead and Clark went past him. As he did, Rawlins put everything he had into one mighty blow that caught Clark on the back of the neck.

A gasp was torn from the big man as he went down on top of the sheriff. He scrambled to his feet, but the speed was gone from him. His face distorted, he snarled:

'Now, I am gonna take you apart, piece by piece . . .'

His hands held out like the paws of a grizzly on two feet, Clark advanced on Rawlins. But the latter saw his great opportunity. He took a couple of quick steps to the side and lunged forward, throwing himself to the ground. He did not quite reach the rifle, but he managed to scramble forward a foot and his clawing right hand brushed the muzzle of the Winchester, then gripped it tightly. He rolled over on his back just as Clark came down on him. Rawlins brought up the stock of the Winchester and smashed it against the side of the giant's head.

Clark cried out in agony, stumbled forward

156

and Rawlins, coming up to his knees, swung the rifle again. The length of it caught Clark on the back and head and he fell to his hands and knees. He could not raise his head, but was not yet unconscious. Rawlins got to his feet, moved forward and coldly, brutally, brought the rifle up and down for the last time.

Clark collapsed on his face. Rawlins threw the rifle aside, reached to within a few inches of Clark's stilled fingers and whipped up the Navy Colt that the sheriff had taken from him earlier that day. He resolved that if Clark regained consciousness again, he would shoot him.

It was not necessary, however. Searching in the sheriff's saddle bags he found a pair of heavy manacles with which he locked Clark's hands behind his back.

It was no use examining the sheriff, but Rawlins, approaching Simpson, found him moaning faintly.

There was still no sign of life inside Lem Goss's store and Rawlins, drawing a deep breath, went inside. He saw Goss at once, lying on his stomach, with his head twisted grotesquely, his neck apparently broken by Clark.

Rawlins made a circuit of the premises. The only horse aside from those ridden by the posse was the single animal in the corral. Rawlins guessed then that Clark's horse had given out and the outlaw had come to the store on foot. That was the reason he was still there.

Rawlins brought the horse from the corral and hitched it to the buckboard. By then Simpson had recovered consciousness. He was barely able to speak. His jaw seemed to have been broken. He managed to get to his feet, however, and watched Rawlins drag Clark's body to the buckboard and boost it into the rear. Rawlins tied Clark's legs securely to the back of the buckboard seat with a length of rope from the store.

He turned to Simpson. 'There's no doctor in Big Springs, I'm sure,' he said, 'and it's at least twenty miles to Ogallala. Think you can make it?'

'Got to,' mumbled Simpson.

Rawlins helped him into the buckboard, found the shotgun with which Clark had killed the sheriff and got some shells from the store. With the reloaded shotgun across his knees, he headed the buckboard north.

It was a long trip to Ogallala. Clark regained consciousness and cursed and thrashed about in the rear of the buckboard, but he was securely tied and Rawlins paid no attention to him. He drove the buckboard at a steady pace and reached Ogallala shortly after seven o'clock. It was still daylight and a small crowd gathered around the sheriff's office as Rawlins got down and went inside.

The deputy recognized Rawlins. 'Hey, you're the Pleasanton man went with the sheriff.'

'The sheriff's dead,' said Rawlins. 'I've got the man who killed him outside.'

The deputy ran past him. Bill Clark had managed to struggle up to a sitting position in the back of the buckboard.

'I can still lick you,' he snarled at Rawlins.

'I'm never going to fight you again,' said Rawlins grimly. 'Not with my bare hands.'

'Damned if I carry this monster inside,' said the deputy sheriff. He drew a knife and cut the ropes that bound Clark's ankles and was narrowly missed by a kick that Clark launched at him.

Rawlins drew his Navy Colt and stuck it into Clark's face. 'Get down and walk inside,' he said coldly, 'and give me an excuse to use this on you.'

Clark kicked a couple of times, then slid back to let his feet touch the ground. He winced, stumbled, but managed to hold his feet. Rawlins' gun was in his back all the way to the sheriff's office and into the cell block. When he was locked inside, the deputy said to Rawlins:

'You'd better go have Doc Williams take a look at you.'

'Simpson needs it more than I do,' said Rawlins. 'I'm going over to the hotel and clean up.'

The deputy started to say something, then shook his head. Rawlins wheeled back. 'Oh—I forgot—there's a sackful of twenty-dollar gold pieces on the buckboard.' He gestured toward the cell block. 'His share of the Union Pacific money.'

The deputy ran past him and by the time Rawlins was outside the deputy already had the heavy saddle bags that had belonged to Clark. 'This ought to make Billy Pleasanton happy,' he said. 'He's been givin' me holy hell ever since he got back here three-four hours ago.'

'He's still here?'

The deputy nodded. 'He wasn't happy about you, either.'

Rawlins nodded thoughtfully and went on to the hotel.

CHAPTER EIGHTEEN

The night clerk was on duty. He stared at Rawlins in astonishment as he came in and headed for the stairs.

Rawlins found his key in his pocket and when he reached the second floor he looked at Room 3. He was tempted to knock on the door, but considered his physical condition and instead went to his own room. He examined his face in the cracked wall mirror

160

over the washstand and peeled off all his clothes.

Using one of the two towels, he washed himself down as well as he could and spent five minutes trying to doctor the bruises on his face. There was one welt that would be swollen for several days, he knew. He was changing his clothing when there was a heavy step outside his door and a fist banged on it.

'Rawlins?' cried the voice of Billy Pleasanton.

Rawlins winced. 'Yes,' he replied.

Pleasanton swung open the door and boomed out, 'I had a wire from the old man. He's got the sheriff of Labette County, Kansas, coming and—'

Rawlins winced and gestured to the thin wall that separated his room from Lucy Paxton.

Pleasanton scowled. 'What's the matter with you?'

Rawlins stepped close to him. 'I don't want anyone to hear you.'

'Why not?' snapped the detective. 'It's open and shut now. You've got Bender in jail and—'

'His sister's next door,' said Rawlins desperately.

'Be damned,' swore Pleasanton. He stared at the wall. Rawlins heard sudden movement through the wall, then a door opened and slammed shut.

161

Lucy Paxton appeared in the open doorway, behind Pleasanton. 'Mr. Rawlins,' she said tartly, 'You've got the biggest surprise of your life waiting for you . . .'

'Hey!' exclaimed Pleasanton, then suddenly pointing at Lucy. 'Kate Bender?'

'You're the big detective,' said Lucy Paxton coldly. 'I've seen you strutting around here today. Well—arrest me and I'll sue you for every dollar your father's earned.' She suddenly bobbed back and went off. Rawlins heard her heels clicking down the stairs.

'Be damned,' said Billy Pleasanton again. 'I talked to her this afternoon. She's singing with Lily Lane at the Trail's End.'

'Lily Lane,' said Rawlins, 'née Molly Johnson.'

'Johnson?' asked Pleasanton sharply. 'I don't think I know . . .'

'Your father's got a thick file on the Johnson boys, I'm sure,' said Rawlins. 'Bloody Bill Johnson, who rode with Quantrill, and his two brothers, Jim and John. Bill's dead, but as far as I know Jim and John are still around . . .' He stopped. 'John . . .'

'Kate Bender,' said Billy Pleasanton. 'I worked with the old man on that case two-three years ago. Yeah, I got the only picture ever taken of old John and his wife, when they first got married. You mean those two lop-eared Dutch produced that?' He

162

pointed toward the doorway, where Lucy Paxton had just been.

'I could be wrong,' said Rawlins wearily, 'but I don't think so.'

Pleasanton reached into his pocket and brought out a telegram. 'Read this.'

The telegram was addressed to William Pleasanton, Ogallala, Nebraska.

Tell Rawlins Sheriff Labette County leaves today. Will be there tomorrow.

Adam

'Station man's got a wire for you, too. He wouldn't let me read it, but it might be important.'

Rawlins reached for his coat. 'I'll walk over and pick it up.' He caught up his Navy Colt and thrust it behind the waistband of his trousers, then blew out the kerosene lamp. Pleasanton was ahead of him, already going down the stairs.

When they reached the street, Pleasanton said, 'I'll mosey over to the Trail's End. Come and show me the telegram, if you think I ought to read it.'

Rawlins walked swiftly to the railroad depot and found the agent about to close up for the night. He looked sharply at Rawlins' battered face. 'Heard you brought in the big fella. Looks of it, he put up a fight . . .'

'Billy Pleasanton said you had a telegram
163

for me.'

'Yes, he wanted to read it, but I wouldn't let him.' The agent scowled. 'His father's nothin' like him. Adam wouldn't ever throw his weight around like . . .'

He opened a drawer underneath his telegraph instrument and took out a telegram. He handed it to Rawlins.

It read:

Charles Rawlins
Ogallala, Nebraska

Sheriff Labette County believes you are wrong, as has information parties went Australia year ago. Believed lost when ship went down near Tahiti all hands missing. However, on my insistence he leaves today for Ogallala. Will arrive there tomorrow. Hope you have time cooperate with Billy on train holdup.

                                        Adam

The station agent said quietly, 'There's talk Billy Pleasanton refused to help Sheriff Whitmore this morning.'

'They had words,' said Rawlins, 'but it was the sheriff's fault as much as it was Billy's.'

'Only Whitmore's dead—and Billy's alive.'

'Lem Goss is dead, too,' said Rawlins. 'You probably never heard of him. He had a little store on the South Platte, below Big Springs,

Bill Clark twisted his head off.'

The telegraph wire began clicking. The agent looked at it in annoyance, then exclaimed and moved to the instrument. He flicked a switch, clicked the instrument a bit and it burst into a continued clatter. The agent whistled softly, then shut off the instrument and turned to Rawlins.

'That was Big Springs. One of the posses caught up with two of the train robbers. They recovered twenty-seven thousand five hundred. They're both dead.'

'Sam Bass?' exclaimed Rawlins.

The agent shook his head. 'One of them didn't die right away. Said his name was Lon Ewing and the other man was called, mmm, Collins.'

'Then Bass is still alive,' said Rawlins, 'and Jim Berry.'

'Ewing was carrying five thousand,' commented the agent, 'Like the man you brought in. But Collins had twenty-two five . . .'

'I guess it wasn't an even five-way split,' said Rawlins. 'When they catch Sam Bass you'll find that he's got twenty-two five, also.' He nodded thoughtfully. 'Jim Berry wouldn't like that split, I'm sure.'

The two men left the railroad depot, the agent locking the door of his office. They walked up the single street of Ogallala, to the sheriff's office. There was a man on the veranda, carrying a rifle, which he brought to the ready as Rawlins and the railroad agent approached.

Rawlins was going in the door of the sheriff's office, when a tremendous roar came across the street from the Trail's End—yells, the stamping of feet and the clapping of hands.

'I'll see you later,' Rawlins said to the station agent and headed swiftly across the street.

The applause continued as he entered the saloon. Lily Lane was on stage. With her was a flushed, excited Lucy Paxton. They wore identical evening gowns and Rawlins had to concede that the woman he believed was Kate Bender was actually more beautiful than Lily Lane.

It was Lily, however, who brought the audience to a semblance of quiet. She kept signaling to stop the applause and finally began singing, which quelled the riot instantly. Lucy Paxton joined her then.

It was the same song that Lily had sung so successfully in Deadwood and she sang it now, as well as she had in the mining town. Lucy sang with her, but it was apparent to Rawlins that Lily was the better singer of the two. Her voice was huskier, her delivery more practiced, her expressions and gestures more natural. But Rawlins' eyes were fixed on Lucy most of the time and it was her voice

166

that he listened to.

Was this girl a murderess?

They finished the song and the applause was even greater than before. Rawlins was reminded of the lack of response the day before when Lucy Paxton, alone, had made her debut in this place.

The two girls finally left the stage and the noise became that of men who were drinking and gambling. The girls were coming down the side of the saloon, passing the bar where they responded smilingly to the comments of the customers. Rawlins saw Billy Pleasanton block them. The girls listened to him and tried to go around him, but the detective continued to block their passage with his huge body. Rawlins started forward and Marmaduke Higgins appeared before him. He had a cheroot in his mouth.

'Lily was in fine voice tonight,' he said to Rawlins. 'That kid with her wasn't bad either.' He clapped Rawlins on the shoulder. 'I heard you brought in the big fellow. He really *was* one of the train robbers?'

'He had his split with him, when I brought him,' said Rawlins. He hesitated. 'I was at the depot a few minutes ago when word came in on the telegraph wire—one of the posses caught up with Joel Collins and Lon Ewing. They had twenty-seven thousand, five hundred dollars on them.'

Higgins whistled. 'I thought I'd get that

kind of money, I'd turn train robber myself.'

'I wouldn't advise it,' said Rawlins. 'Collins and Ewing are dead . . .'

Higgins grimaced. 'And Sam Bass?'

'They haven't caught him yet. They will.'

Higgins used his cheroot to point at Billy Pleasanton, still talking to the two singers. 'That fellow going to catch him? I doubt it.' Higgins frowned. 'He's spilled it you work for the Pleasanton Agency.'

'Adam Pleasanton's the man who wired me the hundred dollars in Deadwood,' said Rawlins, 'but I'm not a regular employee of his. Just on the Bender case, and I've told you that I have a personal incentive there.'

Higgins frowned. 'And you think this Bill Clark is John Bender?'

'I'll know for sure tomorrow. Somebody's coming here to identify him.' His eyes were on William Pleasanton and the two girls, who had finally managed to get past him and were going toward the door.

Rawlins left Higgins abruptly and started for the door. He did not quite reach it. Pleasanton had turned to look after the girls and caught sight of Rawlins.

'Rawlins!' he boomed out. 'Just a minute!'

Rawlins, annoyed, stopped and the big detective lumbered up. 'You got the telegraph from my father?' he asked loudly enough for at least a dozen patrons of the saloon to hear.

Rawlins said, 'Better get over to the

sheriff's office. One of the posse killed Joel Collins and Lon Ewing. They recovered twenty-seven thousand, five.'

'Be damned!' roared Pleasanton. He rushed past Rawlins and slammed through the batwing doors. Rawlins followed, but the big detective was already half-way across the street. Rawlins turned left and saw the two singers just entering the Ogallala Hotel. He hurried after them, but they had already gone up to their rooms when he entered the lobby.

He sat down in the lobby. They were scheduled to sing again at ten o'clock and should be coming down again in an hour or so.

Billy Pleasanton came into the hotel in less than five minutes. His big face wore an unpleasant scowl. 'Damn telegraph man, I'll have his job,' he said. 'Told him I had to send a telegraph and damn if he didn't say he was off duty and couldn't send it until morning.'

'I guess he's got to sleep sometime,' said Rawlins.

'You don't think I let him get away with it, do you?' exclaimed Pleasanton. 'He's over there now, pounding his key. And if he don't sit there and wait until the answer comes back, I'll see that he gets the sack.' He chuckled. 'The Union Pacific's going to be mighty pleased with the agency. Train's robbed in the morning and by night I get back most of the loot.'

Rawlins touched the aching bruise on his face. '*You* got it back?'

'I'm here,' said Pleasanton pompously. 'I'm in active charge of the case. The railroad isn't interested in the details, long's they get the money back.' He smirked. 'Tomorrow, we'll get the other two.'

'Maybe,' said Rawlins. He got to his feet. 'Just thought of an errand. Goodnight, Mr. Pleasanton.'

Pleasanton grunted a response and Rawlins left the hotel. Outside, he stood for a moment, waiting to see if Pleasanton would follow but when he did not, he started swiftly across the street, swerving to the left to go to the railroad depot.

As he approached the depot he saw the light inside the office and heard the clicking of the telegraph key. The door was locked, however, and he had to rap on the window to get the agent's attention. The man held up a finger, finished pounding out a sentence, then came and unlocked the door.

'Got to finish this,' he said and went back to the key. He pounded it for another two or three minutes, listened, then signed off.

'That stuffed moose made me come back and send a telegram to his pa—and then I got to wait until there's an answer. Which may or may not come.' He shook his head angrily. 'Said he'd have my job if I didn't do it.'

'His father isn't like him,' said Rawlins.

'Look, since you're here anyway, would you send a message for me?'

'To the old man?'

'No, it's to someone else.'

'Like you said, I'm here.' The agent handed a pad of message blanks to Rawlins. Rawlins thought for a moment, then began writing. When he had finished he handed the pad to the agent who looked at it and read aloud:

Chief of Police
Rolla, Missouri

Please telegraph description of William Clark, formerly of your city. How long did he live in Rolla. Any relatives. Can you give me details on Sadie Fitch. How long lived in Rolla.

Charles Rawlins
Pleasanton Detective Agency

The agent looked thoughtfully at Rawlins, started to ask him something, changed his mind and moved to the telegraph machine. He sent the message, then turned back to Rawlins.

'Ain't my business, all of this stuff, but if I had some detective business to take care of, I know who I'd hire to do it for me.' He grinned at Rawlins. 'It wouldn't be Billy Pleasanton.'

171

'The man's got an unfortunate personality,' said Rawlins.

'Yeah? Well, look at this.' The station agent shoved a telegraph blank at Rawlins. 'This's what I just sent for him.'

Rawlins started to wave the message aside, then took it. He read:

Adam Pleasanton
Chicago, Illinois

One train robber captured, two killed. Have recovered most of money. Hope to get rest tomorrow. Sheriff Whitmore killed. Can you get authority from governor for me to take full charge here. Wire immediately.

Billy

'What do you think of *that*?' asked the station agent.

Rawlins handed back the telegram. 'Beats me.'

'You got the lumps on your face,' said the agent. 'He takes the credit.'

Rawlins looked at the clock on the wall. It was nine-thirty.

'I hope you get some sleep tonight. Good night.'

Rawlins crossed to the hotel but did not go in. Instead, he walked to the Trail's End. The saloon was filled to capacity, with a staff of

172

four bartenders serving drinks at the bar and several girls and waiters taking drinks to the tables. The games were operating at capacity.

Rawlins found the table at which Marmaduke Higgins was dealing faro and had to wait for at least five minutes before a disgusted player left the game, enabling Rawlins to edge his way up to the table.

'Four loses, queen wins,' droned Higgins. He began to gather in the losing bets and pay out the winning. His eyes suddenly met those of Rawlins.

'Try your luck, Rawlins?'

Rawlins indicated the stacks of bills and currency before Higgins. 'Looks like you're doing all right.'

Higgins shrugged. 'Place your bets, gentlemen. You win some, you lose some.'

Rawlins placed a ten dollar bill on the queen.

'Queen just won,' said Higgins. 'And she's won twice before. I'm telling you because you just got here.'

'I'll let it ride,' said Rawlins. He noted that he was the only player who was playing the queen. The odds were overwhelmingly against a fourth, consecutive win.

Higgins exposed the next two cards and Rawlins noted that he took in more money than he paid out. He noted, too, that the stack of played cards was almost a complete deck. There couldn't be more than four cards left in the box to play and he was certain of it, when money was piled up on the seven by half of the players at the table.

Apparently there was one more seven out and it had lost the last time or two. Odds were in favor of it now. Higgins waited until the players had placed all of their bets, then with his forefinger moved the top card out of the box and exposed a seven.

'Seven loses,' he said smoothly, as curses and angry exclamations arose, 'and . . . queen wins,' he added, moving the seven off the queen.

'Fortune's with you, tonight, Rawlins,' he said pleasantly. 'As it usually is.' The ten dollars that he put on top of Rawlins' money was all that he paid out. He received at least tenfold back on the losing seven.

'And now, gentlemen,' he announced, 'we're down to hock and there's a king and a twospot still left. But which is which, gentlemen? The favorite is the deuce, the king is the longshot . . .'

Money was showered down on the deuce. There were only one or two bets on the king. Rawlins moved his twenty dollars over to the king.

Higgins smirked. 'Again, Rawlins?'

'Again!'

Higgins slipped the cards out of the box. The two was the loser, the king was the winner. Rawlins picked up his forty dollars, thirty of which was profit.

'I'll give it back to you later,' he said.

'With interest, I hope!'

CHAPTER NINETEEN

Rawlins elbowed his way through to the long bar, finding a space close to the stage. He had to wait several minutes for the bartender, then ordered beer. The bartender looked at him in disgust, but finally placed a foaming glass before him.

'Fifty cents,' he said.

'That's twice what it was yesterday . . .'

'Everything's fifty cents tonight. You're payin' for the entertainment.'

Rawlins put down a half dollar and it was whisked away. He sipped the beer and looked at the clock behind the bar. At ten minutes to ten there was a commotion in the front of the saloon, which signaled the entry of the singers.

They worked their way gradually toward the rear, and it took them almost ten minutes to negotiate the fifty or sixty feet. By then the cheering in the Trail's End was deafening and, when the girls climbed up to the stage, they received an ovation that almost tore the roof off.

They began singing and the noise died

175

down. The song was 'Camptown Races,' which Lucy Paxton had essayed on this stage the day before, with disastrous results. But when the girls finished, the applause was even greater, if possible, than that which had greeted them upon their arrival.

It was several minutes before Lily Lane was able to quiet the audience sufficiently to make an announcement. 'My friend is going to sing the next number alone, then I'll join her in a song that we're going to sing especially for every Texan who's here tonight—"Green Grow the Lilacs."'

Stamping on the floor greeted this news, and was still going on when Lily descended from the stage and began to work her way toward the entrance. She saw Rawlins and flashed him a smile as she went by, but Rawlins' attention was on the girl on stage.

Lucy Paxton began to sing. She had confidence now and she sang well. The number she had chosen was a ballad, similar to the one with which Lily Lane had been so successful.

When she finished she received an ovation. The applause may have been a decibel less than she had received with Lily, but it was as satisfying as any entertainer could hope to get. Lucy made her way forward to the edge of the stage and stood there until the applause died out.

'And now,' she announced, '"Green Grow

the Lilacs.""'

It was the song Lily had promised she would sing with Lucy, but now Lucy began it alone. The audience did not seem to mind. Most of the customers were Texans and this was their favorite of all songs; it had been from the time of the war with Mexico.

Rawlins was quite content to listen to Lucy sing alone, but something nagged at him and suddenly it exploded with stunning force. He turned, started rushing toward the front of the saloon. It wasn't too difficult, as men gave way before him, but even so, when he reached the street, it was too late.

Horses were galloping down the street and a badly wounded guard outside the jail was trying to raise himself up sufficiently to send a futile shot at the fleeing riders.

The door of the sheriff's office stood open. Rawlins rushed through the doorway. The door of the cell block was also wide open, and in front of it lay the dead body of the deputy sheriff. At the far end of the room was another corpse, a rifle near its outstretched hand.

Rawlins was surveying the carnage, when an awed voice spoke from the doorway of the sheriff's office.

'Lordalmighty, what's happened here?'

'Jail break,' said Rawlins. He stooped suddenly and scooped up a double-barreled derringer that lay on the floor. 'With a little female help!'

'Female?' The station agent gulped and thrust a sheet of paper in Rawlins' direction. 'Hey—I was just takin' this to you at the hotel. Thought you'd want to see it.'

Rawlins snatched the telegram from the agent. It read:

Charles Rawlins
Pleasanton Detective Agency
Ogallala, Nebraska

No one named Sadie Fitch ever lived in Rolla. William Clark lived here for a few months working as blacksmith. Killed man with bare hands and fled. When last seen was six feet six inches, weight two hundred fifty pounds. Glad to be of service to your agency.

Harlan Tompkins

Rawlins stared at the telegram and read it a second time. He was still looking at the flimsy sheet of paper when Billy Pleasanton burst into the room, from the street.

'My gawd!' he cried, 'what happened here?'

'What does it look like?'

Billy Pleasanton put the toe of his big boot against the body of the deputy sheriff. He turned him over. 'It's the deputy. That means there's no law left in this town.' His eyes fell

178

on the station agent. 'What the hell *you* doin'
here? Didn't I tell you to stay at the depot?'

'Yes sir,' gulped the agent, 'but I had to—'

'You had to, nothing,' snapped Pleasanton.
'Get your tail back there and the minute that
message comes through from my father, you
bring it to me. Understand?'

'Yessir. Where, uh, where'll you be?'

'Here! Where else? I've got to organize a
posse.' His eyes went to Rawlins. 'Look,
Rawlins, you brought him in and . . .'

'Once was enough,' said Rawlins grimly.
He headed for the door.

'Wait!' cried Billy Pleasanton. 'Where are
you going?'

'To take care of some private business.'

'That can wait. This is the important thing.
I've got to get a posse together and
somebody's got to lead it.'

'You're in charge,' said Rawlins. '*You* lead
it.'

'I can't. I've got to take care of things
here.'

'Go ahead. I'm sure your father can get you
the authority now . . .'

Rawlins walked out of the sheriff's office,
on the heels of the station agent, who began
trotting back toward the railroad depot.

Rawlins went swiftly across the street,
passed the hotel and went on to the Trail's
End. Lucy Paxton was nowhere in sight.
Rawlins wheeled back to the door and

179

returned to the hotel.

He climbed to the second floor, went at once to the door of Room 3. A thread of light showed under the door. Rawlins caught the doorknob, tried it, but found the door locked.

'Open up,' he said.

There was silence inside the room and he rattled the doorknob. 'Who is it?' called Lucy Paxton.

'Open up,' snapped Rawlins. 'Open up, or I'll break the door down!'

He gave the doorknob another rattle and then heard the bolt being shot back. He slammed the door open, almost hitting Lucy Paxton. She exclaimed angrily and wheeled toward the bed, on which lay an open, partially packed valise. She thrust her hand into it, but Rawlins sprang forward, gripping her by the shoulder, and swung her violently away from the bed.

Lucy cried out and struck at him with her clenched fist, catching Rawlins squarely on his cheekbone and stinging him, so that he automatically struck Lucy with his open hand. It was a hard slap and brought a cry of pain from the girl. She threw herself at him and he struck her again with his left hand, rocking her head.

'You want to fight like a man you'll be treated like one,' raged Rawlins. He caught her by the left shoulder, shoved her back violently, so that she slammed against the wall. She remained there, gasping from her own anger and Rawlins' fury, as he fished a .32 Colt from her valise and faced her.

'They're gone,' Rawlins said savagely. 'They got away. They left three dead people behind them, but what the hell are three, more or less?'

'What are you talking about?' cried Lucy Paxton.

'Your friend Lily Lane.' Rawlins whipped the double-barreled derringer from his pocket and thrust it under Lucy's face. 'She went into the jail and got the drop on the deputy sheriff.'

'Oh, no!' wailed Lucy Paxton.

'Tell me you weren't in on it?' sneered Rawlins. He stabbed the derringer at the suitcase on the bed. 'Then why were you packing?'

'Because I . . .' Lucy stared at Rawlins. 'Lily . . . killed a man?'

'What's one dead man—or three? *You've* killed twenty-three!'

'No, *no*!' wailed Lucy Paxton. 'It isn't true. I . . . I never . . .' She stopped, her eyes fixed on Rawlins. 'I know . . . you've made enough cracks about it. You think I'm . . . Kate Bender . . .'

'Well, aren't you?'

A shudder seemed to run through her but she regained a measure of composure. 'If you

181

think I am—arrest me!'

'I'm not a policeman,' said Rawlins. 'But I am holding you here until one arrives—and that'll be tomorrow morning. And you know who it'll be? The sheriff of . . . Labette County, Kansas.'

'I've never been in Labette County, Kansas, in my whole life.' She shook her head. 'Your sheriff's going to make a long trip—for nothing.'

'I don't think so.' Then he added skeptically, 'But even if he does, that doesn't mean you're out of it. There's no law here now, but sooner or later that thick-headed Bill Pleasanton is going to put two and two together and figure out that you and Lily were in it together—you to hold the crowd in the saloon, while Lily went out and sprung Clark from jail.'

'I had nothing to do with that,' cried Lucy. 'Believe me, I didn't!'

'And if Billy Pleasanton doesn't figure it out, his father will!'

There was concern on Lucy's face. 'Look,' she said, 'I can't talk you out of believing that I'm—I'm Kate Bender, but I'm not worried about that, because *I* know I'm not and it'll work out. But please—believe me, I had nothing to do with . . . with what happened across the street. Lily . . .' She faltered.

'Yes?' prodded Rawlins.

'She's helped me before and she said she

was going to help me tonight—she'd get the
audience all steamed up, then she'd let me
sing alone. She said it was the one way to let
me prove myself.' She looked at him
miserably. 'You saw what a flop I was
yesterday, but tonight . . . with Lily, they
seemed to . . . to like me.'

'*I* liked your singing,' conceded Rawlins.
'What I don't like is . . . who you are . . .
what you've done.'

Lucy sighed. 'All right, think what you
like. Now, let me alone. I'm tired.'

Rawlins let out a snort of disdain. 'Uh-uh,
not again!' He crossed to the door, closed it
and shot the bolt. Lucy cried out in alarm,
'What are you doing?'

Rawlins picked up the single chair in the
room, placed it with its back to the door and
sat down. 'If you think I'm going to let you
out of my sight for one single minute before
the man from Labette County gets here . . .'

'But you can't stay here—in my room!'
cried Lucy.

'Watch me,' said Rawlins.

'Lock me in,' she said. 'Stand outside if
you like, but . . .'

'And let you climb out of the window?
Uh-uh . . . it's about eleven hours until the
westbound train comes in tomorrow morning.
That's how long I'm going to wait here . . .
eleven hours.'

'That's impossible,' wailed Lucy. 'I've got

183

to go to bed . . .'

'I won't stop you.'

'There are things a person has to do . . .'

'If you mean you've got to go to the toilet.'

'You're a bastard,' snapped Lucy.

'The little room's across the hall,' said Rawlins. 'You can go anytime. The window in it isn't big enough to climb through, so I'll know you're safe enough while you're in there.'

'Mr. Rawlins,' said Lucy furiously, 'I'm going to bed!'

She stepped to the bed, slammed shut the suitcase and put it on the floor. She threw herself upon the bed, and deliberately folded her arms across her chest and closed her eyes.

Rawlins exhaled heavily and settled down for a long siege.

CHAPTER TWENTY

There was comparative quiet in the room for awhile. Lucy's breathing was heavy and regular, but diminished gradually. From where he sat Rawlins could not see much of her face, but his eyes roamed over her form. She still wore the red evening gown that matched the one worn by Lily Lane.

Rawlins scowled as he wondered if Lily were riding in the evening gown. She'd had to move fast after leaving the Trail's End and there had been no time for her to change her clothes. Of course, the jailbreak was a prearranged plan and she had probably had a change of clothing stowed away, ready for the getaway.

But . . . why Lily? Why not Lucy? If Bill Clark really was John Bender, it would only have been natural for *her* to have helped her brother to escape. And she would have gone with him.

Not necessarily. Kate Bender had been a fugitive for three years. She was used to every subterfuge, every wile, that a desperate, hunted woman could think of. Her condition was with her every waking moment—even in her sleep she could not relax entirely.

Look at her now, lying on the bed while a man was in the same room with her. She was relaxed, oblivious . . . or, was she?

Rawlins said, quietly: 'Bill Clark's your brother.' She made no reply and he went on. 'He fits the description I got in Labette County and it was verified by the chief of police of Rolla, Missouri.'

She opened her eyes, but did not look toward Rawlins.

He said. 'You knew I'd be watching you, not her, so you worked it out that way.'

'Mr. Rawlins, shut up, I want to sleep.'

She closed her eyes again and once more her breathing became heavy as she pretended to sleep. She would not sleep, though, Rawlins knew that. Nor would he, for he was wider awake now than he had ever been. He would be just as wide awake when the gray light of dawn seeped into the little room.

An hour went by. Footsteps had sounded on the stairs and in the hall two or three times, as guests went to their rooms. Now, heavy boots clumped up the stairs, stopped at the door of the adjoining room. Knuckles rapped loudly on the door.

'Rawlins, it's me, Billy Pleasanton. I want to talk to you.'

He knocked on the door again, rattled the doorknob, then clumped back to the steps and down.

Lucy spoke then. 'How does it feel to be a detective, Mr. Rawlins? Can you look at yourself in the mirror every morning?'

'I imagine I can look at myself easier than *you* can look at *yourself*,' retorted Rawlins.

'That's precisely the answer I expected,' said Lucy. 'From you.' She suddenly sat up in bed and swung her feet to the floor. For a moment she stared at the floor, then raised her head and looked squarely at Rawlins.

'Mr. Rawlins,' she said, 'look at me. Do I look like a murderess?'

'No, you don't. But maybe that's how you got away with it. And I guess it's the reason no one really got close to you in the past three years. That, plus the fact that you did what

186

no one would expect you to do. Instead of burying yourself in a hole somewhere, you got out in public—became a singer and appeared on a stage where everyone could look at you. Was that your idea or Lily Lane's?'

'As a matter of fact,' said Lucy, 'it was Lily's suggestion. I was working in a millinery store. 'I've supported myself since I was twelve years old.'

'At twelve you were still with your family.'

Lucy sighed wearily. 'My father died when I was three, my mother when I was seven . . .'

'Where?' asked Rawlins mockingly. 'Where did your mother die? In the Blake Street prison in Kansas City?'

'Yes. She was killed when the building collapsed . . .' Lucy stopped. 'You don't believe me, of course.'

'I don't believe you,' said Rawlins, 'because the story you're telling me is that of Molly Johnson.'

Lucy lowered her head and stared at the floor for a long moment, then she raised her head again, but did not look at Rawlins. 'In Chicago,' she said, 'when you first asked me my name, I was angry and—made a slip. I blurted out the name of Molly Johnson.'

'You said that it was the first name that came into your mind.'

'Yes, but do you know why?'

'Tell me.'

'Because it was my real name.'

He laughed, but there was no humor in it. 'I could see that coming.'

'I knew you wouldn't believe me.'

'Kate Bender,' said Rawlins, 'I've been on your trail for three years. I got your description from a dozen people in Labette county. I've hunted for you in Kansas, in California, in Texas. I've thought of you every waking hour for three long years. Every time I'd see a pretty face, I'd look at it and wonder—is this Kate Bender? When you got on the streetcar in Chicago, I thought you were the most beautiful girl I'd ever seen. That was the way I thought of Kate Bender and when I saw you I asked myself immediately, could this be Kate Bender? Then I saw the way you handled yourself. You clouted that drunk with your fist. You didn't ask for any help—you handled a tough situation by yourself. Well, that was the way I thought Kate Bender would handle herself.'

'Of course,' said Lucy, 'after killing twenty-three men, one drunk more or less . . .'

Rawlins went on. 'The name Molly Johnson meant nothing to me, then. But I followed you. You told me you were staying at the Palmer House, but you went into the Potter Hotel—and promptly disappeared. I thought at first you'd gone in one door and

188

out the other, but I talked to the bell captain. He knew you right away . . . said you were registered as Miss Lucy Paxton. That's when I got suspicious . . . but not *really* suspicious yet. Until I saw you again and you gave me the slip—climbing out of your window, going down the rope fire escape. You were desperate to get away from me . . . why? Because I look like my brother, whom you murdered in Labette County? I went through your room and I found something in your wastebasket, a torn-up letter . . . only it wasn't torn up the way most people tear up an old letter. It was shredded to bits. But you'd have been better off to eat the scraps, or burn them. I put them together. It was a letter from someone named John to his sister.'

'Of course,' said Lucy. 'My brother John.'

'John Bender.'

'John Johnson,' said Lucy. 'I had two older brothers. Bill and Jim. They were both killed during the war . . . like my mother.' She paused for a moment. 'I don't know how you learned about the Blake Street Prison.'

'Adam Pleasanton put me onto it. Then I talked to the officer who was in charge of the prison, Captain Tom Leach. He's got a stiff leg now and he's running a little pipe and tobacco shop in Kansas City. He kept a list of all the prisoners and I saw the name of Molly Johnson there, and . . . Kate Bender. You knew each other then and I guess you kept in

189

touch, so that when . . .'

'Mr. Rawlins,' said Lucy. 'Mr. Adam Pleasanton has the reputation of being the smartest detective in the country—and I guess you've learned some lessons from him. But neither one of you did a good enough job in Kansas City. You missed something.'

'What?'

'You didn't investigate the children well enough. If you had, you'd have discovered that there was a little girl in the Blake Street Prison who was singing all the time, who had an excellent voice even at that age . . . and knew how to deliver a song. Her name was . . . Kate Bender.'

'Exactly,' said Rawlins. 'I heard you sing.'

'But you've also heard Lily Lane sing,' said Lucy. 'Now, be honest, who's the better singer? Lily . . . or me?'

Rawlins looked at her closely.

Lucy said, 'Didn't they tell you in this Labette County that Kate was always singing?'

'The Benders didn't live in Labette County that long. The short time they were there, they were busy . . . killing the people who came into their restaurant. And I happen to know that it was Kate who brought people into the place. My brother wrote me a letter once. It was just gossip, but I remember what he said. You want to hear it?'

'I'm listening to everything else—why not?'

190

'He wrote, "There's a German family moved in near Cherryvale. I've passed there a couple of times; the old man and the old woman are nothing much and the son's just an overgrown lout, but they've got a daughter—whew! She's only sixteen now, but if you visit me sometime in the next couple of years and she hasn't been grabbed up yet, I think you'll be settling down here."'

'Well, she *is* beautiful, isn't she?'

'You're still trying to point the finger at Lily. What I just quoted from my brother's letter—I memorized it. Nothing was said about her voice, about her singing all day, which she would have had to do to sing the way Lily does now.'

'Charles,' said Lucy seriously, 'the things you've told me yourself and things Lily's said about you—you were in the Union Army during the war—in western Missouri. You know about Quantrill . . . and the men who rode with him.'

'I know they were a murdering bunch of bushwhackers who used the war for their personal vendettas, their thievery . . .'

'You still feel that way, although the war's been over for eleven years?'

'I have no reason to change my mind. Look at the James boys, the Youngers—they're still at it.'

'And the Johnsons,' said Lucy quietly. 'I was seven years old in 1863, but they put me

191

in jail along with my mother, because . . . because of what my brothers had done. Bill and Jim . . .' she laughed, without humor. 'Bloody Bill Johnson, they called my oldest brother. He had the ears of six human beings on his bridle reins when he was killed. But that wasn't the way *I* knew my oldest brother. I remember him as . . .' She made a gesture of dismissal. 'All right, if you still think that way about guerrillas, what about the *other* people? After my mother died I was put in the Jackson County Home. Some people named Paxton took me, finally, but they made me take their name and then it got out that I was the kid sister of Bloody Bill and after a while they brought me back to the Home. I was there six months and to get rid of me they sent me east, to Rolla, where I was adopted again. I kept the name Paxton and nobody identified me as the sister of the Johnson boys . . . but *I* knew it—and I *still* know it!'

Rawlins said, 'You've got that pretty speech well memorized, haven't you? Did you rehearse it . . . with Molly Johnson?'

A groan was torn from Lucy's throat. 'I've said what I had to say, that's all, Mr. Rawlins. Good night.'

She swung her feet up from the floor and dropped back on the bed. She remained silent and after a long while Rawlins thought she was sleeping, but he was not sure. He did not sleep himself. He sat on the straight-back chair for hours. Once or twice he got to his feet, stretched himself for a few moments, but then seated himself again.

CHAPTER TWENTY-ONE

It was a long night. On the bed, Lucy turned several times, but she did not open her eyes or speak and Rawlins did not talk to her. He thought, however, during those long hours. He went over what she had said to him, the things he knew, and as the night wore on he began to have doubts. He shrugged them off, but they came back.

The dawn finally began to seep into the room and Rawlins got carefully to his feet and stepped to the wall lamp. He turned down the wick, then looked at Lucy Paxton. She was lying on her side, her mouth slightly open. Her breath came evenly and Rawlins knew that she was asleep.

He went back to his chair.

Light began to fill the little bedroom and soon the sun shone in, illuminating Lucy's body and her face.

A slow sigh came from her lips. She opened her eyes and suddenly sat up. She swung her feet to the floor, looked at Rawlins and covered her face with her hands.

'I had a terrible dream,' she said, then took her hands away. 'I'm hungry. Do you intend to starve me, too?'

'No,' said Rawlins. 'I didn't want to wake you up, but if you want to go across the hall, now . . .'

'I do.'

'I'm going into my own room. I'll be gone ten minutes. It'll give you time to change your clothes. But move around, so I can hear you.'

'I'll make noise,' said Lucy.

'Then we'll go downstairs and have breakfast.'

Rawlins removed the chair from the front of the door and then shot back the bolt. He went to his own room, leaving the door slightly ajar and was able to hear Lucy Paxton cross from her own room to the little one across the hall.

Rawlins washed himself quickly, but did not shave. Then he sat down on the bed and waited. He heard Lucy return to her room, opening and closing drawers. She was probably not using them but wanted to make enough noise so that Rawlins would know she was in the room. He waited a good ten minutes, then he heard her door close and a knock on his own, still opened, door.

'I'm ready,' she announced.

She had changed her dress, combed her hair and looked as fresh and attractive as she

194

always had. The long, difficult night seemed to have left no impression on her.

The dining room had just opened and they were the first for breakfast. They gave their order to the waitress, who brought them coffee while the rest of the order was being cooked. Lucy drank greedily.

'I'm not good in the morning until I have my coffee,' she said. Then she rested her elbows on the table and looked at Rawlins.

'What have you decided, Mr. Rawlins?'

'I've decided that I don't like being called Mr. Rawlins.'

'Well, how about *Detective* Rawlins?'

'My name is Charles, which you know damn well.'

'Very well, Charles, and what will you call me—Lucy? Or . . . Kate?'

'I'll try Lucy . . . until I learn definitely otherwise.'

'You mean, you're not so *sure*, this morning?'

'I was sure that Bill Clark was John Bender.' Rawlins drew out the telegram he had received the night before from the chief of police of Rolla, Missouri. He smoothed it out and shoved it across to Lucy.

Lucy glanced at it. 'Sadie Fitch.' She grimaced, read the rest of the telegram and frowned.

'Who's Bill Clark?' asked Rawlins.

'As far as I know, he's—Bill Clark.'

'You know him?'

She hesitated, then nodded. 'He lived in Rolla for a while. When Kate—when Lily came to visit me she met him and they, well, they had a brief affair. Then Clark got into a fight with a man—over Lily—and killed him.'

Rawlins drew a deep breath. 'Where's your brother John?'

'In Deadwood,' she said, then added; 'I think. I hear from him once or twice a year. I've only seen him three or four times since I was a child. I never saw him at all from the time—the time Mother died—until four or five years ago, when he showed up in Rolla and introduced himself. He didn't stay in Rolla very long and I hardly got to know him.'

'But he keeps in touch with you? How?'

'His letters are usually forwarded—and I write him once in a while to give him a new address. He's been in Deadwood since early winter.'

'What does he do there?'

'It's a mining town, isn't it? He said he had a claim. Not a very good one, though.'

'You've said it before,' said Rawlins heavily, 'but tell me once more; Bill Clark *isn't* your brother?'

'I told you—he's a murderer!'

'Of course, that's a bad word. You wouldn't have anything to do with a murderer.'

196

'That sarcasm's in your voice again, Mr. Rawlins.'

'Charles!'

'*Mister* Charles. You were a Union soldier, the other side were all murderers. My brother Bill, John . . .'

'We won't talk about them,' said Rawlins, 'not until . . .' He stopped as the waitress brought them their breakfast. She bustled about for a few minutes, straightening things on the table, seeing that they had tableware and condiments. As she left, Billy Pleasanton came into the dining room.

'Here you are, Rawlins,' he boomed. 'I tried to find you last night, but you weren't in your room.'

'No,' said Rawlins, 'I wasn't.'

'I heard from my father about midnight. He said the governor was issuing an order putting me in charge here. It came just a little while ago.' He smirked. 'I've already got two posses out. One of them went out right after midnight. I had to promise to pay ten dollars a day to every man, which'll probably have to come out of my own pocket.'

'Or, your father's.'

'It's the same thing,' said Pleasanton. 'In his telegram, he said to ask you to help me.'

'We settled that last night.'

'The old man won't like it. He said—' He made a gesture of dismissal and pulled out a chair. 'Miss Paxton, like to ask you a few

197

questions, about your vaudeville partner, Lily Lane.'

'Yes?'

'I have reason to believe that Miss Lane was an accomplice to the jailbreak last night. This ought to interest you, too, Rawlins. If the big fellow, Clark, was really John Bender, couldn't this, ah, this Lily Lane be his sister, Kate Bender?'

'You've got the one picture of her father and mother in St. Louis. You've seen Miss Lane—does she look anything like either of her parents?'

'I haven't seen the picture in a long time. Besides, if I remember right, that picture was twenty-some years old. It was the wedding picture of the Benders.' Pleasanton scowled. 'Miss Paxton, just how well did you know Lily Lane?'

'Quite well, or rather I *thought* I knew her well. She came to my home town three years ago. She'd just started singing and she wanted a partner. She listened to my voice and suggested we go on a tour, as a team. We tried that for a little while, but it didn't work out too well. Lily . . . Lily's a much better singer than I'll ever be and the managers wanted Lily, not Lily and a second-string singer.'

'You sang all right last night,' said Pleasanton. 'I liked you about as well as the Lane woman.' Then he caught himself. 'You

198

said you started out as a team three years ago, then split. How come you joined up again?'

'Our split was professional only. We remained friends and we saw each other every now and then. We even played a few dates together. I had a letter from her a couple of weeks ago and she asked me if I'd be interested in joining her here. Of course, I seized the opportunity, especially as I—I needed the money.'

Pleasanton frowned, then turned to Rawlins. 'They told me that Miss Lane came down here, direct from Deadwood. That's where you came from, too. Did you—did you happen to know her there?'

'Yes, I did. I also knew Bill Clark there.'

'But you never saw the two of them together?'

'On the contrary, I *did* see them together. And they seemed very friendly.'

Pleasanton shook his head. 'Thing bothers me about you, Rawlins, you know everybody, singers, road agents . . . murderers . . .'

He pushed back his chair. 'Some other questions come up, I'll talk to you later, Miss Paxton.' He frowned at Rawlins. 'They brought in those fellas from Big Springs, Collins, uh, Ewing.'

'And the gold?'

'They brought that, too.' He suddenly brightened. 'Them two, last night, they was in such a danged hurry they forgot to pick up

199

the five thousand gold Clark had on him when I, uh, when *you* brought him in.' He shook his head. 'The old man won't like you refusin' to help.'

He went off. Rawlins looked after him. 'Give him a day or two more and he'll actually believe that *he* shot it out with Collins and Ewing.'

'He practically said that he captured Clark.'

'I caught that.'

'Mr. Rawlins,' said Lucy, 'Charles! Thank you for not telling him your—your suspicions about me.' A little shudder ran through her. 'I don't think I'd like to be in jail with him . . . with him in charge.'

'The man's a pompous oaf, a stuffed shirt.' Rawlins drank the last of his coffee and put down his cup. 'If you've finished . . .'

'Do we have to go upstairs now?' cried Lucy. 'It's so nice outside.'

She stopped, her eyes going past Rawlins. The latter turned. Marmaduke Higgins was bearing down on them.

'It pays to get up early,' chuckled Higgins. He pulled out the chair that had just been vacated by Billy Pleasanton. 'Miss Paxton, what do you think of what happened last night?'

'She just got through telling Billy Pleasanton,' said Rawlins.

'I thought he'd be out chasing the bandits by this time,' said Higgins.

'He's sent out two posses. He's in charge—in official charge. His father pulled some strings with the governor and Billy Pleasanton's the law in Ogallala, in the whole county, for that matter.'

'That means we'll have Pleasanton men all over the place,' said Higgins. He sent a quick glance at Lucy. 'No offense, Rawlins.'

'I'm not a Pleasanton man,' said Rawlins. 'It's all right, Miss Paxton knows about me. But for your information, I quit the agency job. I quit when Billy began to throw his weight around.'

Higgins nodded. There was a slight frown on his face. 'Miss Paxton, apparently you've known Lily Lane for some time. Did you have any suspicion that she might be . . .' He looked at Rawlins. 'I'm sure you've considered that yourself, Rawlins. That—'

'That Lily Lane is Kate Bender?'

'She knew John Bender in Deadwood, remember? You almost had a fight with him because of it.'

'I could have made a mistake,' said Rawlins, carefully. 'I assumed that Clark was John Bender . . .'

'You had some reason to suspect him—you told me yourself you had information that Bender was in Deadwood. All right, if he and Lily were so thick—it figures in view of what happened last night that she was his sister' He turned suddenly to Lucy. 'What do *you*

201

think? *You* knew her better than anyone else.'

Rawlins said, 'You know somebody for years and then something happens and you realize you didn't really know that person at all.'

'You ought to know the Bender family by now,' said Higgins. 'You've been on their trail long enough. What do you think—is Lily Lane Kate Bender?'

'I'll ask you. You were on the stage with her from Deadwood to Fort Pierre. Then you came downriver together and out here by train.'

Higgins grinned. 'I played poker just about every minute I was on the boat. Like I told you, I won eight hundred dollars. Which is just about what I made yesterday, my first day in Ogallala.'

'I knew a faro dealer in Texas,' said Rawlins, 'In fact, I arrested him . . .'

'Arrested!' exclaimed Lucy. 'I thought you said you weren't really a detective at all.'

'I was a Texas Ranger for a year,' said Rawlins. He nodded to Higgins. 'I think I told you that.'

'You did. This faro dealer you started to tell about?'

'He showed me a little trick. Claimed it was invented by a retired faro dealer who sold the trick to other dealers . . . for five thousand dollars.' He looked at Higgins who was showing great interest. 'He had a prepared deck,' Rawlins went on. 'There was a tiny hole, just about the size of a pinpoint in four of the cards. A bit of horsehair went through the holes in the four cards and was tied together. With a good false shuffle these four cards remained at the bottom of the deck. It's quite an advantage for the dealer to control the last four cards, isn't it?'

'That's when the big money's bet by those who're watching the cards.'

'Like last night, when I played at your table. Not that I'm suggesting *you*'d do a thing like that.'

'Of course not. But you got those cards tied together. How you going to slip them out one at a time if they're tied together?'

'Oh, that's the rest of the trick. The box has a very sharp point inside. When the deck is pressed against the point, it cuts the horsehair.'

'Be damned,' said Higgins. Then he was aware of Rawlins' steady gaze and began to smile. 'I didn't pay five thousand dollars for it. I'd appreciate that you didn't spread that around. Not while I'm still here.'

The waitress came up to take Higgins' order and Rawlins looked at Lucy and pushed his chair from the table. 'It's almost time . . .'

'Time for what?' asked Higgins.

'The westbound train's due in a few minutes,' said Rawlins.

'Who're you expecting on the train?'

Lucy said, 'He's expecting the sheriff of Labette County, Kansas.'

Higgins stared at Rawlins in astonishment. 'But she's flown the coop. She's a hundred miles from here by now.'

'I've still got to meet him,' said Rawlins. 'You want to come along?'

'Not me,' said Higgins. 'I've never been overly fond of sheriffs.' He smiled thinly. 'I've had my troubles with them. Go ahead, have a good visit and send him back to Lafayette—no, what is it? Labette!'

As they started across the street, Rawlins was aware of Lucy's nervousness.

'It'll be over in a little while,' he said.

'I hope so,' said Lucy, but she could not help adding, somewhat fearfully, 'How could he remember Kate after all this time? He might—he *might* make a wrong identification.'

'You've convinced *me*,' said Rawlins. 'I think you can convince him.'

They reached the sheriff's office across the street, where a new guard was now posted. He carried a Winchester, as the guard of the night before had. They passed the livery stable, then crossed to the railroad depot.

There were more than a dozen townspeople already on the railroad platform to come to meet the train. The station agent was pulling a four-wheeled cart from the baggage room to the edge of the platform. He saw Rawlins and came forward.

'Mr. Rawlins, where's Junior?'

'Junior?'

'Billy Pleasanton. The old man's coming in on the train. Sent a wire from Platte City. I just delivered it to the big oaf.' He sent a scowl over his shoulder. 'I got one hour's sleep last night. The old man keeps Billy on the job here, I'm going to quit.'

The whistle of an approaching train was heard and far to the left an engine appeared on the tracks, coming around a sweeping curve. It was a long train, with four passenger and several freight cars. Rawlins looked quickly at Lucy, standing beside him. Her face was strained.

Billy Pleasanton joined them on the platform. 'Here you are, Rawlins. I just got word that the old man's on the train. Glad to get this chance to talk to you before he shows up.' He scowled. 'You aren't going to tell him I had nothing to do with getting those train robbers yesterday?'

'That's between you and your father—and your conscience,' said Rawlins.

'He's going to believe me, anyway,' said Pleasanton huffily. 'The only thing you can do is make trouble for yourself.'

'Billy,' said Rawlins, 'do me a favor, will you? Go over there and don't bother me. I've got my own troubles.'

Glaring at Rawlins, Pleasanton moved away, standing as near the edge of the tracks as he could, without stepping down on them.

The engine passed the depot, and then the mail and express car and the first two passenger cars. Billy Pleasanton began to move along with the train, peering at the windows. He was determined to get to his father before anyone else could.

But he missed. The train stopped and people began getting down from each car. At the far end of the platform from the last passenger car, a familiar figure stepped down and Rawlins began moving toward him.

'That's Adam Pleasanton,' he said, 'and,' he looked sharply at the slight, middle-aged man who had gotten off directly behind Adam Pleasanton, 'the sheriff of Labette County.' Rawlins touched Lucy's arm and she went forward with him.

Adam Pleasanton caught sight of them. 'Rawlins,' he exclaimed, 'you heard I was coming?'

He thrust out his hand and they shook hands. Releasing Rawlins' hand he said, 'Here's someone you may remember. Sheriff Hudspeth of—'

'Yeah, sure,' said the man beside Pleasanton, 'I remember you.' He thrust out a lean hand. 'Where's this murderin' female that you brought me all the way from Kansas to see?' His eyes flicked from Rawlins, to

Lucy, then back to Rawlins.

'You're looking at her,' said Rawlins.

'Hell,' snorted Sheriff Hudspeth, then caught himself. 'Excuse me, miss.' He shook his head angrily. 'This don't look nothin' like the Kate Bender I knew. I seen that little murderess once I seen her twenty times. She don't look like you at all, uh-uh!'

Adam Pleasanton said, 'Sorry, Rawlins. I was afraid you were making a mistake.'

'To finish it up, sheriff,' said Rawlins, 'can you describe John Bender? Is he . . . a man six feet, six inches tall . . .'

'Hell, no. He's big but not much bigger'n you. Strong, yeah. He had to be to swing that ax . . . Excuse me, miss.' Sheriff Hudspeth drew a deep breath.

'Like I told Mr. Pleasanton on the train, I got this telegram from San Francisco a year ago and I went all the way out there. This clerk at the shipping office had come across one of the copies of the old picture I'd distributed, the one of old John and his wife when they was first married. Feller said he was sure he'd sold them tickets on the *Hola Maru* that'd sailed two weeks before. He described them pretty good, not the way they looked in the picture, but the way they was the last time I saw them myself. Said their English was—well, mostly Dutch. Like I told Mr. Pleasanton, the ship went down with all hands lost. I'm satisfied the whole family

207

went down, because if their pa and ma was on the ship, so were the young 'uns.'

Billy Pleasanton came lumbering up. 'Dad,' he cried, 'I been looking for you!'

'Billy,' said the old detective, giving his offspring a hard look. 'I thought you'd be out with the posse.'

'I was with them yesterday, all day, but after I took charge here, I thought I'd better . . .' His eyes went to Rawlins. 'What you been tellin' him, Rawlins?'

'I've told him nothing, Billy,' said Rawlins.

Adam Pleasanton took his son's arm. 'Let's go and have us a little talk, Billy.' He started to lead Billy Pleasanton away, then caught sight of Sheriff Hudspeth. 'Sheriff, if you'll join us . . .' He nodded to Rawlins. 'I'll see you before I leave.'

The three men left and Rawlins looked at Lucy. She seemed to be shaking from suppressed excitement.

'I apologize,' he said, 'for last night . . .'

'Don't,' she cried. 'I'm so glad, so . . .' She stopped, caught Rawlins' arm and clung to it in relief.

They started after the three men ahead of them, but slackened their pace so they would not catch up to the Pleasantons and Sheriff Hudspeth.

CHAPTER TWENTY-TWO

The liveryman had brought out a fine bay mare and was grooming her in front of the stable. Lucy suddenly said:

'I wonder why she didn't want me to go riding with her yesterday?'

Rawlins' mind was on other things, but he caught her remark and said, 'Who?'

'Lily. She rented a horse yesterday and when I offered to go riding with her she said she preferred to ride alone.'

They had passed the livery stable and Rawlins wheeled back. He approached the liveryman.

'Did you sell a couple of horses yesterday afternoon?'

'That's my business,' replied the liveryman. 'You take this animal here, she's as good a mare as you'll find in the state. Ain't been rid by no danged cowboy, neither. The way they treat their horses is a crime.'

'The horses you sold yesterday—did a woman buy them?'

The man hesitated. 'She paid cash on the barrel, didn't try to beat down the price. She tried out one horse and when she came back . . .'

'I'm talking about Miss Lily Lane,' said Rawlins, 'the singer who appeared at the

Trail's End yesterday.'

'I know,' said the liveryman. 'Billy Pleasanton gave me holy hell this morning. Blamed me for helpin' the train robber escape. Hell, I on'y sold the horses. How was I to know what they was going to be used for?'

'When she took the horse out earlier in the afternoon, how long was she gone?'

The liveryman rubbed his stubbled chin. 'She gave him a good workout. I had to rub him down afterwards. Mm, two hours, I'd say.'

Rawlins looked inquiringly at Lucy. She nodded. 'Perhaps a little less than two hours.'

The liveryman clapped his hand on the bay mare. 'Here's a horse that's worth more'n those two I sold yesterday. I could let you have her for only a hundred, uh, a hundred and twenty-five dollars.'

Rawlins turned to Lucy. 'You've got some riding clothes you can wear?'

'Yes.' Eagerness lit up her face. 'You mean, we could go riding?'

'As soon as you change your clothes.'

She started for the hotel, went a few feet, then stopped. 'Aren't you coming with me?'

'I'll wait here.'

Lucy ran across the street to the hotel. Rawlins turned to the liveryman.

'Saddle up the mare . . .' he looked into the stable, 'and the roan gelding there.'

'You mean you're going to . . . buy?'

'Maybe later. We'll try them out first. Don't worry—if I don't buy, we'll pay rental.'

The liveryman's face fell. 'Got to charge you five dollars apiece.'

Rawlins reached into his pocket and brought out a ten dollar gold piece. The liveryman brightened and took the money. He led the mare into the stable, got a saddle and threw it on her. Rawlins walked back to the entrance and looked across the street, toward the hotel. He started to cross the street, but turned back. The liveryman finished saddling the two horses, brought them out and tied them loosely to the hitchrail. 'Any time you're ready, mister.'

It was more than ten minutes since Lucy Paxton had entered the hotel. She had dressed very quickly in her room earlier.

Rawlins waited another two minutes, then started across the street. He had just reached the hotel door, when Lucy came out. She was wearing riding half-boots, Levi's and a flannel shirt.

'You were coming for me!' she said.

'No,' said Rawlins, then changed his answer. 'As a matter of fact, yes.'

'I went into Lily's room,' said Lucy. 'Her riding clothes are still there.'

'She was in a hurry last night,' said Rawlins. 'She could only count on four or five

211

minutes' head start.' He stopped, staring at Lucy. She nodded.

'She didn't intend to ride very far,' said Lucy. 'Not in that—that tight evening dress.'

Rawlins caught Lucy's arm, gripped it hard. 'She knew there'd be pursuit.' He thought for a moment. 'It fits the pattern. When she skipped from Labette County, she didn't go into a hole. She—she went to the big cities, appeared in public. Where no one would be looking for her.' He turned to look up the street, toward the east. 'She rode off in that direction last night. Do you remember which way she went riding earlier?'

Lucy pointed to the east.

Still gripping Lucy's arm, Rawlins pushed her in the direction of the hotel. 'Go back, wait for me.'

'No,' said Lucy, 'I'm going with you.'

'There may be gunplay.'

Lucy shook her head. Rawlins shrugged. He led the way to the livery stable and when they reached the horses at the hitchrail, he turned to help Lucy up into the saddle. It was not necessary. She put a foot into the stirrup and vaulted up easily, lightly. The stirrups were a little too long for her but she did not seem to mind. Rawlins untied the reins from the rail and mounted the roan gelding. In a moment they were galloping up the street, headed east.

As they left Ogallala proper Rawlins heard

a train whistle and saw an eastbound Union Pacific train rolling along.

The road on which Rawlins and Lucy rode was well-worn, but there were few houses in sight after they left the outskirts of the town itself. There was a cattle ranch on the north side of the road and across the tracks in the distance Rawlins saw cattle grazing on the sparse vegetation, but after riding for three miles they saw no more cattle or buildings, only a desolate landscape.

Rawlins did not know what he was looking for, but he kept his eyes steadily on the edge of the road, hoping to find signs that horses had turned off the main road. He could find no tracks and was becoming anxious after they had gone about four miles.

The road dipped ahead and crossed a small stream, which had been bridged to the width of a single wagon. The stream itself was shallow at this time of the year, but the banks were high, indicating that the water was fairly deep at times. The stream continued to the south, where a railroad trestle had been built over it.

Rawlins was riding across the little bridge, when he stopped his horse, turned and rode back. He dismounted and, moving to the edge of the bridge, studied the ground. There were no signs that horses had turned off the bridge and gone down into the water. He looked at the south side as well, then remounted and continued across the bridge. He kept his horse at a walk as he examined the sides of the road.

He found what he was looking for almost a hundred feet beyond the bridge. There were hoofprints leading off the road to the south. With Lucy following, watching him closely, Rawlins dismounted and bent over to follow the tracks. It was not easy. There were clumps of heavy salt grass that at times obscured the tracks, but he persevered and followed the tracks to the very edge of the railroad grade. There the tracks turned west and went on to the little stream.

Rawlins rode into the water and crossed the stream. As nearly as he could tell, there were no hoofprints on the westerly side. The horses had gone either upstream, or down, under the railroad tracks.

Lucy moved up beside him and Rawlins sat his horse, debating which way to turn. North? South?

North led into the dry lands, the unknown country between southern Nebraska and the Black Hills. Rawlins had come from that direction only a short time ago. He knew how desolate the country was. It was an ideal place for an outlaw hideout. But Kate Bender had always taken the obvious path. He turned his horse to the south, bending low as they rode under the trestle. They rode for a mile, in the water. In some places it was no more than an inch or two deep, and in others almost two feet. At one point the water reached the horses' bellies.

They rounded a turn in the creek and saw an ancient structure that stood on the bank of the stream. It was an old soddy house, built many years ago by an early settler in western Nebraska and later abandoned. There were no windows in the building and the door hung from a single hinge. There was no sign of life.

Rawlins pulled up his horse and studied the soddy.

'Stay here,' he said to Lucy in a low tone, then rode his horse out of the creek bed. There was heavy grass on the bank, but it was virgin grass and seemed untrodden by beast or man, at least, not within recent years.

Rawlins drew the Navy Colt from his waistband, and holding it at his right side, urged his horse toward the soddy.

Then a voice called to Rawlins. It came from his right, the direction of the stream.

'Now, just stop right there, Mister Rawlins! And drop that there gun you got in your fist, because if you don't—'

Rawlins' first impulse was to swing to the right and begin shooting, but his native caution stopped him. It was well that he had not. He turned his head slowly toward the creek and saw Bill Clark, his upper body exposed from behind the bank, with a

Winchester rifle at his shoulder, aimed at Rawlins. The big man had a happy expression on his face.

'You ain't dropped the Navy gun,' he said. 'I ain't ready to kill you just yet, but if you don't drop her . . .'

Rawlins dropped the gun. He was fairly caught and had no chance for a shot.

'Yeah, now, that's all right,' cried Bill Clark. He rose and climbed up the river bank. 'Now, if you'll just step down from that plug . . . on this side!'

Clark wheeled suddenly to the left, fired his Winchester. 'You!' he roared. 'C'mon up and join the party!'

The bullet had been fired at Lucy Paxton, who now began to ride forward. Bill Clark began to chortle. 'There's a friend a your'n at the soddy, missy. I'm sure she'll be glad to see you again.'

He gestured with the Winchester at Rawlins, who began to close in on the soddy house. He was fifty feet from it, when a bent figure came through the hanging door.

It was Lily Lane. She had discarded her evening gown and now wore Levis and a wool shirt. Both garments looked new. She held a businesslike shotgun in her hands.

Her eyes, for the moment, were not on Rawlins, but on the girl who came up from the rear. 'You bitch,' she said, addressing herself to Lucy, 'you'd still be making old

216

ladies' hats in that whistle-stop if I hadn't given you the opportunity to make something of yourself.'

'You used me,' said Lucy. 'You needed someone to draw attention away from you. It had to be someone who was ashamed of her own name, like me. You used me to cover up your tracks, your identity . . .'

The big man with the Winchester began to chuckle. 'Now, now, girls, let's not you two start fightin'. 'Cause I got a little fightin' to do myself . . . eh, Rawlins?'

'I'm not going to fight you again,' said Rawlins.

'The hell you ain't. You didn't fight fair yesterday.'

'No, Bill,' said Lily Lane. 'We're not going to take any chances at this stage of the game.'

'Chances? What chances? You'll be holdin' a shotgun on him.' Clark suddenly grinned. 'Or, better yet . . .' He put two fingers into his mouth and whistled a piercing blast. His eyes went to the door of the soddy.

A man came out. He too was holding a Winchester.

It was Marmaduke Higgins.

'Surprised, Rawlins?' he called out mockingly.

'Not too much,' said Rawlins. 'Somebody *had* to show her this place yesterday— somebody who'd been in Ogallala before. And somebody had to bring her out those

217

new clothes this morning.'

'Very good,' said Higgins. 'You may make a detective after all. Someday. That is, if you . . .'

'Charles,' said Lucy suddenly. 'This man is . . . ?'

'John Bender,' said Rawlins simply. His eyes went to Lily Lane. 'What happened to your father and mother?'

Higgins said carelessly, 'Who gives a damn? All I know is they left the country.'

'They did,' said Rawlins. 'They started for Australia, but never got there. The ship went down with all hands.'

For one instant, a sober, almost tragic, look came over Higgins' face, but then he shrugged. 'Just as well.' He came forward. 'All right, Bill, if you've *got* to fight . . .'

Bill Clark threw the Winchester aside. 'Man to man,' he said to Rawlins. 'No holds barred!'

Higgins cried out. 'Damn it, Bill, watch yourself.' He rushed forward and scooped up the Winchester. He held one in each hand; Rawlins made a mental note of that. Higgins would be encumbered for quick shooting. But Lily Lane still held the shotgun gripped in both hands. She was watching him with a bitter, almost savage, look on her face.

But Rawlins could not let his attention wander from Clark. The giant was advancing on him, his hands held at shoulder height, the

218

fingers of each hand spread into huge claws. He was ready to strike, maim or gouge, and Rawlins dreaded the coming moments. He did not think he would survive. Although, if he did . . .

A man does not die willingly, however. No matter how futile, he will fight to the last ounce of his strength. Clark came at him in a rush and Rawlins, suddenly bending forward, threw himself violently against the big man, hitting him with head and shoulders, partly turned sideward. He struck low in the stomach and the force of Clark's rush carried him over, on top of Rawlins. Rawlins heaved up as Clark hit him and spilled the man over his shoulders, onto the ground on his back. Clark fell heavily, but scrambled over to his hands and knees. He was not quick enough to dodge the savage kick Rawlins got in to his face.

Clark let out a roar of rage and came up. Blood was gushing from his mouth and he began swearing. Rawlins, backing away from the giant, found himself within a foot or two of the muzzle of the shotgun in Lily's hands. She jammed it forward, striking him in the back.

'Get back, you coward,' she jeered.

Coward? With two people holding guns on him, with a superman coming in on him with lethal hands and arms?

Clark was on his guard now. The flying

tackle of a moment ago would not work again. But Rawlins could not retreat or sidestep. He could only go forward. He rushed in, swinging with both fists. He caught Clark on the cheekbone with his left fist, sending a shock of pain up to his elbows. He followed through with his right, landing on Clark's face. His hand came away smeared with blood. He struck again at Clark's face, and the blood on his fist caused it to skid off the big man's face and past his ear.

Clark took hold of him and Rawlins knew again the agony of the bear hug that he had known the day before, in their first encounter. Clark buried his face in the side of Rawlins' face and shoulder, making it hard to hit him. He locked his hands behind Rawlins' back and squeezed. In desperation, Rawlins tried to kick the big man. It was like trying to kick steel posts.

The roaring came again to his ears. It was punctuated by a dull explosion and he was aware of the gasp that was torn from Clark's lips against his face.

The grip on Rawlins had gone suddenly slack.

Rawlins brought his hands up, tried to force them between himself and Clark—and succeeded. There was another dull explosion, followed by a thunderous roar, and Clark suddenly reeled back.

Rawlins had one wild glimpse of Lucy

Paxton. She stood several feet away, a short-barreled revolver in her fist—the gun Rawlins had found in her suitcase the night before. She had gathered it up when she had gone to her room to change her clothes.

The gun thundered again—and Lily Lane née Kate Bender, fell over, face down.

Rawlins wheeled, and saw John Bender sitting on the ground, trying desperately to lever a fresh cartridge into the chamber of his Winchester. He was having difficulty, for there was a wound on the side of his forehead from which blood poured into his eye.

Rawlins staggered away from Clark, who stood flailing his hands furiously as he tried to move forward again, to follow Rawlins.

Rawlins saw something on the ground near the prone body of Kate Bender—the shotgun that had fallen from her dead hands. He rushed forward, stooped and scrambled to turn around. He heard the big man lumbering toward him, threw himself on his back and brought up the shotgun. He pulled the trigger and Clark's face seemed to disintegrate into blood, gristle and bone.

Clark stood for a moment, swaying back and forth; then, like a stricken oak tree, he crashed to the ground.

Rawlins got up to face Higgins, but the gambler had fallen over on his side. Rawlins walked over to him. John Bender's eyes were open, but glazing. Rawlins was still looking down at him, when he heard sobbing nearby.

Turning, he saw Lucy Paxton, the revolver dangling from her hand, her bosom heaving with great sobs. Tears streamed down her face.

'I shot them,' she said, 'I shot them all . . . one after the other . . .' Suddenly she became aware of the gun in her hand and threw it away.

'It's all right,' said Rawlins, walking toward her.

Lucy said, 'I'm just like my brother . . . Bloody Bill Johnson . . .'

'It's all right,' said Rawlins. 'It's all right.' He took her into his arms and it was all right, then.

For both of them.

Photoset, printed and bound in Great Britain by
REDWOOD BURN LIMITED, Trowbridge, Wiltshire